P9-DND-036

*A life-threatening journey promises
untold riches...for those who survive*

A BOOK FOR:

Mrs. Kowar

FROM:

Maciej
Andrejczyn.

Scholastic
Book Fairs®

Jason set the rifle against a tree and walked close. The antlers were so broad, he might not be able to touch from one side to the other with arms outspread.

Suddenly the moose blinked, and a hind leg twitched. It was still alive! Before Jason had time for a second thought, the moose was on its feet and charging.

Jason looked over his shoulder. The moose had its head down, about to gore him with those sharp tines, when the husky came flying. The moose turned its antlers toward the dog instead, and flung King aside like a rag doll.

A moment later the hooves rained down again, a shot rang out, and then all was darkness.

# Awards for
# *JASON'S GOLD*

## Other books by Will Hobbs

# JASON'S GOLD

## WILL HOBBS

HarperTrophy®
*An Imprint of HarperCollinsPublishers*

Harper Trophy® is a registered trademark of HarperCollins Publishers Inc.

Jason's Gold
Copyright © 1999 by Will Hobbs
Map illustrations by Virginia Norey

Library of Congress Cataloging-in-Publication Data
Hobbs, Will.
    Jason's gold / Will Hobbs.
        p.    cm.
    Summary: When news of the discovery of gold in Canada's Yukon in 1897 reaches
fifteen-year-old Jason, he embarks on a 5,000-mile journey to strike it rich.
    ISBN 0-688-15093-4 (trade) — ISBN 0-380-72914-8 (pbk.)
    1. Klondike River Valley (Yukon)—Gold discoveries—Juvenile fiction.
[1. Klondike River Valley (Yukon)—Gold discoveries—Fiction.   2. Voyages and
travel—Fiction.   3. Orphans—Fiction.]   I. Title.
PZ7.H6524Jas   1999                                                          99-17973
[Fic]—dc21                                                                        CIP
                                                                                   AC

First Harper Trophy edition, 2000
❖
Visit us on the World Wide Web!
www.harperchildrens.com

*for my brothers,*
*Greg, Ed, and Joe*

St Michael

Arctic Ocean

Yukon R.

ALASKA

UNITED STATES

CANADA

Mackenzie R.

NORTHWEST TERRITORIES

Dawson City

Yukon R.

Stewart R.

Skagway

Juneau

Pacific Ocean

N

Liard R.

Great Slave Lake

Fort Chipewyan

Edmonton

CANADA

Vancouver

Seattle

UNITED STATES

PACIFIC NORTHWEST
• 1897 •

0                    500
Scale in Miles

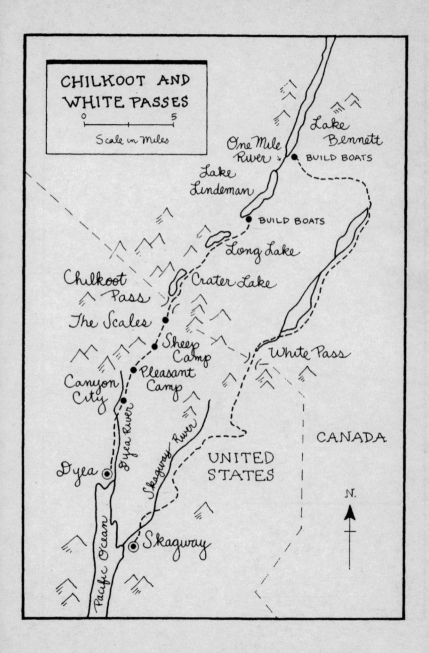

CHILKOOT AND WHITE PASSES

0       5

Scale in Miles

Lake Bennett

One Mile River

BUILD BOATS

Lake Lindeman

BUILD BOATS

Long Lake

Chilkoot Pass

Crater Lake

The Scales

Sheep Camp

White Pass

Canyon City

Pleasant Camp

Dyea

Dyea River

Skagway River

CANADA

UNITED STATES

Pacific Ocean

Skagway

N.

# Contents

PART ONE

# Klondike or Bust

## ONE

When the story broke on the streets of New York, it took off like a wildfire on a windy day.

"Gold!" Jason shouted at the top of his lungs. "Read all about it! Gold discovered in Alaska!"

The sturdy fifteen-year-old newsboy waving the paper in front of Grand Central Depot had arrived in New York only five days before, after nearly a year spent working his way across the continent.

"Gold ship arrives in Seattle!" Jason yelled. "EXTRA! EXTRA! Read all about it! Prospectors from Alaska. Two tons of gold!"

The headline, GOLD IN ALASKA, spanned the width of the entire page, the letters were so enormous.

People were running toward him like iron filings to a magnet. He was selling the *New York Herald* hand over fist. His sack was emptying so fast, it was going to be only a matter of minutes before he was sold out.

1

"Prospectors from Alaska arrive in Seattle! Two tons of gold!"

Jason wanted to shout, Seattle is where I'm from! but instead he repeated the cry "Gold ship arrives in Seattle," all the while burning with curiosity. Beyond the fact that the ship had arrived this very day—this momentous seventeenth of July, 1897—he knew nothing except what was in the headlines. He hadn't even had a chance to read the story yet.

It was unbelievable, all this pushing and shoving. A woman was giving a man a purse-beating over his head for knocking her aside. "Skip the change!" a man in a dark suit cried amid the crush, pressing a silver dollar into Jason's hand for the five-cent newspaper. "Just give me the paper!"

When there was only one left, Jason took off running with it like a dog with a prize bone. In the nearest alley, he threw himself down and began to devour the story.

*At six o'clock this morning a steamship sailed into Seattle harbor from Alaska with two tons of gold aboard. Five thousand people streamed from the streets of Seattle onto Schwabacher's Dock to meet the gold ship, the* Portland.

Five thousand people at Schwabacher's Dock! He knew Schwabacher's like the back of his hand. Mrs. Beal's rooming house was only six blocks away! Were his brothers, Abraham and Ethan, among the five thousand? Maybe, but probably not. At that hour they would have been on their way to work at the sawmill. Would they have risked being fired for arriving late? He didn't think so. His older brothers were such cautious sorts. Hurriedly, Jason read on:

*"Show us your gold!" shouted the crowd as the steamer nosed into the dock.*

*The prospectors thronging the bow obliged by holding up their riches in canvas and buckskin sacks, in jars, in a five-gallon milk can, all manner of satchels and suitcases. One of the sixty-eight, Frank Phiscator, yelled, "We've got millions!"*

Jason closed his eyes. He could picture this just as surely as if he were there. He'd only been gone for ten months. Suddenly he could even smell the salt water and hear the screaming of the gulls above the crowd. Imagine, he told himself, *millions in gold*. His eyes raced back to the newsprint:

*Another of the grizzled prospectors bellowed, "The Klondike is the richest goldfield in the world!"*

*"Hurrah for the Klondike!" the crowd cheered. "Ho for the Klondike!"*

*Klondike*. Jason paused to savor the word. "Klondike," he said aloud. The name had a magical ring to it, a spellbinding power. The word itself was heavy and solid and dazzling, like a bar of shiny gold.

*One of the newly rich disembarking the ship was a young man from Michigan who'd left a small farm two years before with almost nothing to his name. As he wrestled a suitcase weighing over two hundred pounds down the gangplank, the handle broke, to a roar from the crowd.*

It almost hurt reading this, it was so stupendous. Two hundred pounds of gold!

That man had left home with almost nothing to his name, Jason thought, just like I did. That could have been *me* if only I'd heard about Alaska ten months ago, when I first took off.... It could have been Jason Hawthorn dragging a fortune in gold off that ship.

Jason could imagine himself disembarking, spotting his brothers in the crowd, seeing the astonishment in their eyes . . . their sandy-haired little brother returning home, a conquering hero!

"Dreams of grandeur," he whispered self-mockingly, and found the spot where he'd left off:

> *A nation unrecovered from the panic of '93 and four years of depression now casts its hopeful eyes upon Alaska. Today's events, in a lightning stroke, point north from Seattle toward that vast and ultimate frontier whose riches have only begun to be plumbed. It may well be that a gold rush to dwarf the great California rush of '49 may already be under way as these lines are penned, as untold numbers of argonauts, like modern Jasons, make ready to pursue their Golden Fleeces. Klondike or Bust!*

The rush is only beginning, he realized. It could *still* be me.

A grin was spreading across his face. A modern Jason he already was, and in fact his father had named him after the treasure-seeking hero from Greek mythology.

In a split second all his plans were turning about like a racing sloop. His sails were filling with a wind blowing from an entirely different direction.

Then he hesitated, remembering the vow he'd made to himself to live on his own hook for a year before returning home. But ten months was nearly a year, he reasoned, and he knew from his brothers' letters and telegrams that they were already impressed by his stamina and resourcefulness, as well as by the marvelous mountains and prairies and cities that he had seen.

Just think how it would strike Abraham and Ethan if he returned from the road only long enough to pack up and light out for the Klondike!

"It's the roving bee," his father always used to say, "that gathers the honey."

Jason broke into a wide smile remembering his father, who had dreamed of breaking the bonds of "wage slavery" and becoming his own boss. His father had never realized the dream himself, but he had passed the vision on to his sons. Though they'd deny it, Jason thought, his older brothers had already given up, resigned themselves to a lifetime of wage labor. Jason himself had vowed he never would.

He couldn't afford to spend another minute as a mouthpiece of history while others were rushing to *make* history. Time was of the essence. With a fortune in gold, he could fulfill his father's dream in one bold stroke.

He collected his packsack from the rooming house where he'd been staying and set out for Seattle. It didn't matter that he couldn't afford a ticket—he'd hobo his way back. This gold rush had his name written all over it. He'd head home to Seattle, then somehow . . . north to Alaska!

## TWO

Who could have imagined, who could have hoped there'd be another gold rush? Unthinkable, that there was an overlooked last frontier where a fortune could be made overnight simply by pounding a claim stake in the ground.

Yet suddenly, like a comet, it was upon them, and tens of thousands found themselves ripe for adventure. The Wild West was going to have one great last act after all.

The entire continent, in a matter of hours, came down with Klondike fever, or "Klondicitis," as it was soon dubbed. Within a day, people were heading west from small towns and big cities all across the United States and Canada. Most were coming by railroad; some were even setting out on bicycles.

At first there was a great deal of confusion about the exact location of the Klondike goldfields. A newspaper in Memphis, Tennessee, reported that the Klondike was not far north of Chicago. But the telegraph wires were soon humming the true destination: Dawson City, a boomtown of three thousand souls that lay fourteen hundred miles up the Yukon, the great river of the North. The name Klondike came from the small, clear-running Klondike River, which joined the Yukon at Dawson City. To the surprise of millions, the goldfields were not in Alaska at all, but in Canada.

Everywhere, families were deciding who would be the ones to go—mostly their young men—and were making it possible by pooling their resources. Great-aunts and great-uncles who'd hoarded gold pieces under the floorboards during the hard years were suddenly offering their life savings without hesitation. Why not, when the gold in the creekbeds was "thick as cheese in a sandwich," as described by the Klondike's celebrated American discoverer, George Washington Carmack? Some people were even grubstaking strangers who'd placed ads in the classifieds.

Only two days after the arrival of the much-heralded gold ship, the first steamer left Seattle filled with stampeders headed for Skagway, Alaska, a settlement of only two buildings at the edge of an immense wilderness few could imagine. Once in Skagway, the Klondikers would begin carrying all their supplies over the mountains to the goldfields. The little steamer, named the *Alki*, set sail from Seattle crammed with 900 sheep, 65 cattle, 30 horses, 350 tons of supplies, and 110 passengers, the first droplets of the human tidal wave that was to come.

Jason Hawthorn was desperate to get in on it. After four days of riding the rails he'd reached Minot, North Dakota, where he found himself in extremely cramped quarters. Jason was sharing a boxcar with hundreds of bags of flour headed for the Klondike trade in Seattle and two men who looked like blown-in-the-glass hobos. The younger man, who sported a Buffalo Bill goatee, was swilling whiskey from the bottle and reciting, endlessly, the popular jingle about a purple cow. The old one, a grizzled fellow who was on his way to the Klondike but looked as if he'd just come back, was hacking at his overgrown beard with a long, sharp knife and tossing the severed clumps of gray out the open door of the boxcar.

Jason had a Minnesota newspaper to read, which took his mind off the drunk and the purple cow and his own growling stomach. He hadn't eaten since St. Paul.

The paper was full of news from Seattle, beehive central for the staging of the rush. Seattle's mayor, Jason read, had been in San Francisco when the gold ship had arrived with its millionaire prospectors. The mayor immediately wired home his resignation and started buying and chartering steamships and selling tickets to the north. In only a few days, twelve of Seattle's policemen had resigned. Clerks were walking off their jobs; barbers were dropping their straight razors, leaving men half-shaved. Doctors deserted their patients; the streetcars hadn't run since the gold ship had docked. Seattle's newspaper, the *Post-Intelligencer*, had declared, "Prosperity is here! So far as Seattle is concerned, the depression is at an end."

In California, mines were shutting down because their workers were rushing off to the Klondike to make their own fortunes. Fruit pickers were walking away from their ladders.

The young whiskey-swiller next to Jason, in an

inebriated fit of inspiration, started to sing the cow
jingle while waving his arms like a conductor:

> *"I never saw a purple cow,*
> *I never HOPE to see one;*
> *But I can tell you, anyhow,*
> *I'd rather see than BE one."*

With this, the fellow suddenly threw up on Jason's
leg.

Jason cursed softly, cleaned his trousers as best he
could with his bandanna, then tossed the bandanna out
the side door. He accepted the effusive apologies of the
drunk but moved closer to the old man and fresh air,
though it crowded both of them.

"I believe we just met the purple cow himself," the
old man said wryly. "And I agree, I'd rather see than *be*
one."

"Excuse me, but I overheard you telling this fellow
that you're bound for the Klondike?"

"Wouldn't miss the last dance for the world," the old-
timer said with a smile punctuated by missing teeth.
"I'da been about your age when I first left home in the
Blue Ridge Mountains of North Carolina. Tramped all
the way to California."

"You were there in '49?"

"Nearly fifty years ago . . . and a few rushes in
between . . . in Colorado, the Black Hills of South
Dakota, the Cariboo of British Columbia . . . yessir, I have
*seen* the elephant."

"Seen the elephant? I . . . I don't understand."

"Never heard that expression before, have you? It
was what everybody was saying—every man, woman,

and child—on their way to the California rush back in
'49. Yessir, we was all 'going to see the elephant.'"

"But what does it mean?"

The old-timer grinned, eager to spin his tale. "It's
from an old story. . . . There was this farmer, you see, who
had heard about elephants but never seen one. All his
life he'd hoped to get the chance. Well, finally one summer he heard that a circus, complete with an elephant,
was visitin' a nearby town. That farmer heaped his
wagon high with milk and eggs and vegetables of every
kind to sell at the market there, and headed off with high
hopes.

"On the way, he met the circus parade, led by none
other than the elephant. The farmer was delighted, but
his horses were terrified. They started to buck, and
wildly. The wagon pitched over and all his valuable pro-
duce hit the ground—a complete loss. When the man got
back home, he told his wife and friends what had happened. They tried to comfort him about losing his pro-
duce, but, to their surprise, the man cried out, 'Oh, no!
Don't be sorry! I don't give a hang—for I have *seen the
elephant!*'"

The old-timer's weather-beaten face was creased
with laughter as he finished his story. Jason wasn't sure
he knew what to make of this tale, so instead of saying
so, he announced proudly, "I'm heading for the
Klondike, same as you."

"Well, then, you're going to see the elephant."

## THREE

The old-timer would have regaled him with another story, but advice on practical matters was what Jason really wanted. "I've been scouring the newspapers trying to figure how much it'll cost to outfit myself for the Klondike once I get home to Seattle. Do you have any idea?"

The old man combed his newly shorn beard with his fingers. "Five hundred dollars, I'm hearing, will buy you everything—a thousand pounds of food, all your clothing, a sled, a gold pan, and a pick and a shovel. It'll even get you a 'Klondike stove,' as they're callin' them little cookstoves, and saws and nails and oakum for boat-building once you reach the headwaters of the Yukon."

Jason's heart almost burst with anticipation. "Five hundred is exactly what my father left me—my brothers

11

never let me touch it when I quit the cannery last
September."

"Took off cross-country, did you?"

"That's right. My brothers were sure I'd be back in
two weeks, with my tail between my legs."

"But here you are," the old man said with a gravelly
chuckle. "You and me, we're cut from the same cloth.
Nope, you shouldn't miss the Klondike. So your father's
deceased, is he?"

"He died four years ago, when I was eleven, from
scarlet fever. Right after he passed away I started working in the cannery. My mother died before I could even
remember her. So it's just me and my brothers now, but
they're much older than I am. They work at a sawmill in
Seattle, but the owner of the mill won't hire you until
you're sixteen, so I could never work there. Too dangerous, he said. As if it was safe at the cannery! Once, a kid
standing next to me lost two fingers."

"What kind of hours you work?"

"Ten hours a day, six days a week. It was the best-
paying job I could find, so I never quit. I helped pay the
bills for three years, and I'm proud of that."

"Here's to the exploiters of labor," the old-timer
declared with heavy sarcasm, hawking up a mighty wad
of phlegm and spitting contemptuously out the boxcar
door. "How much did the captains of industry pay you?"

"Ten cents an hour. I got to where I despised the
work so much—the stink of fish too—every minute felt
like an hour."

"Don't blame you a bit."

"I'm never going back to the cannery or any kind of
factory. I'm going to be on my own, work for myself.
That's why I have to strike it rich."

"Maybe you will, kid, maybe you will."

"A Klondiker needs to take a thousand pounds of food, you said? Can that be right?"

"It's an empty country up there. Got to take everything with you, sounds like. The entire outfit should weigh nearly a ton, they're saying."

"How is anyone going to carry a ton of supplies over the mountains? I read that the portage is thirty or forty miles."

"A little bit at a time, they say, or you hire packers if you have the money—Indian packers or horse packers. Or you bring your own horses."

Jason's mind was spinning with calculations, and now he started talking it through to the old-timer. "My brothers each inherited the same as I did, $500. If they'd just stake me an additional $250 each, I'd have $1,000. That should be enough, don't you think?"

"I imagine it would be."

"I would promise to cut them in for a third each of my fortune. Each would be risking $250 against the probability of hundreds of thousands in profits."

"I hope they see it your way."

"So do I. Our father hated gambling as much as he did drinking, but this would be an *investment*. I just have to convince my brothers to see it that way. They're like bumblebees in tar, sometimes. They get so stuck in what they're doing. If they don't agree, I'll just have to figure out how to get there on my own."

The old-timer suddenly nodded off to sleep, and in a few seconds, he was snoring. Though exhausted, Jason couldn't sleep. As he watched the prairies roll by, his dreams and his worries simmered together in a mulligan stew.

One way or another, he would get there.

Jason lost track of the old-timer in the train yards of Helena, Montana. More and more men were converging on the trains headed west, and it was a mad scramble to find a place to hide.

As the train topped the Cascades and mighty glacier-capped Mount Rainier appeared on the horizon, Jason's imagination came to a full boil. He rode belly-down atop the mail car, with the forests and rivers flying by, cinders burning holes in his clothes. "Klondike or bust!" he was hollering. "Ho for the Klondike! Watch my smoke!"

It had taken him eight days to cross the continent. Late in the evening of July 25, the train pulled into the Seattle yards.

Seattle had been transformed. Despite the late hour, the streets were clogged with thousands of men, women among them, and sometimes children, too. Their supplies were stacked ten feet high along the sidewalks. Outside of every restaurant, there were long lines in the street. Steerers moved among the crowd, enticing people toward the stores, and every store window screamed the magic word *Klondike:* Klondike soup, Klondike boots, Klondike stoves, Klondike glasses, Klondike blankets, Klondike picks and shovels.

Confusion and excitement reigned.

Klondicitis!

With a high heart, Jason made his way to Mrs. Beal's rooming house. He was home from the road and his brothers would be home from the sawmill. In a matter of minutes he'd be meeting up with them. He was taller by several inches than when they'd seen him last, broader across the shoulders, his voice was deeper. He would remember not to make big of himself, especially around Abraham, his oldest brother, who was always so serious and slow to give approval, slow to say much on any subject.

Abraham . . . tall and rawboned, like the legendary martyred president he was named for. Clean-shaven, though, except for a mustache. Jason remembered Abe's slight limp, and the story of how he came by it before Jason was even born. "Streetcar winged him," their father liked to say, but Jason could never really picture it. The accident might explain Abraham's cautious approach to everything.

And then there was Ethan, who was said to favor their mother's side of the family. Dark-haired, the only curly-head in the family, with a full beard since he was sixteen. Ethan's impish green eyes came to mind, his hearty laugh. Ethan, always the teaser. You never knew if he was serious or kidding until he gave you the wink and the nod. Though he was as strong as a prizefighter, Ethan always deferred to Abraham in matters of judgment.

It was Jason who'd been born with the ferocious independent streak. "I can do it on my own!" had been his battle cry since anyone could remember. His brothers wouldn't be surprised when he told them he'd decided to be a Klondiker. They would realize he was perfectly suited to go north, and they'd back him all the way.

Jason knew he could find a way to make it happen. "Don't let anything stump you," their father had always said. "You can do whatever you set your mind to."

He couldn't dwell too long on his father, or he'd be teary-eyed the next second. His recollection of his father's face after four years was blurry at best, and that scared him. All he had in the world now were his two brothers, and he'd already run off on them once to prove he could make it his own way.

As he neared the boardinghouse, he was remembering a conversation they'd had nearly a year ago.

"Why didn't you tell us how bad it was at the cannery?" Abraham had asked soberly when Jason announced he was leaving home.

"Because he's stubborn as a halibut," Ethan had answered. "You know he never complains."

"We can find you another job," Abraham insisted. "Or you don't even have to have a job. You like to read so much . . . maybe we could afford for you to go to school. Surely you don't intend to drift wherever the wind takes you."

But Jason had held his ground. "The wind blows from west to east," he'd told them, "and I intend to visit Gettysburg and lay my eyes on the Atlantic Ocean."

Well, he'd done both of those, and learned something of half a dozen trades along the way. It hadn't been easy. So many times, lonesome and hungry and broke, he'd thought of turning heel, but he hadn't. And now he was returning home, no worse for wear, even though he had only two dollars in his pocket. He hoped his brothers would be proud of him.

Jason remembered with regret the harsh things he'd said when they tried to dissuade him from leaving. "You just have no imagination," he'd told them, his words rushing out as if from behind a broken dam. When he saw the hurt on their faces, he'd wanted to call the words back, but it was too late. Many times during these long days and months he'd been away, Jason had vowed he would show them, when he next got the chance, how much they really meant to him. They were everything to him, these big brothers. Now he would tell them in person.

Jason's heart was in his throat as he burst through the front door and straight into the common room.

They weren't there. The room was crowded with men, but his brothers weren't among them. The landlady, Mrs. Beal, was at her desk.

"Jason!" she cried. "You're back!"

"Are they in their rooms?" he asked breathlessly. "My brothers?"

"Lord no, Jason! They've gone to Alaska!"

He went dizzy, as if he'd been blindsided with a left hook. "My brothers? What? When did they leave?"

"The day before yesterday! So much has been happening around here so fast, it's impossible to keep up with!"

"I can't believe it. *My* brothers? My brothers went to *Alaska*?"

"Oh, everybody's got Klondike fever. They came down with a severe case, Jason. Made up their minds as they were watching the prospectors disembark from the *Portland* with all that gold, I'd guess."

"They saw all that? They were there?"

"Even I was there. It was the most exciting thing I ever hope to see. It's a wonder the entire population of Seattle didn't drop dead from excitement. Here, Jason, they've left you something."

Mrs. Beal reached into a drawer and brought out a letter.

Jason didn't know what to think. He was numb all over as he began to read.

> Seattle, Washington
> July 22, 1897

*Dear Jason,*

*I write on the eve of a momentous adventure. Ethan and I are in the midst of frenzied preparations for our departure to the Klondike. We are in possession of two tickets for the steamer* Falcon, *sailing tomorrow evening for Skagway. Ethan and I find ourselves in the enviable position of leaving in the first week of the rush. We intend to race to Dawson City and stake our claims at the head of the pack. We will be among the first to claim the prize!*

*Unfortunately, we are unable to inform you of our plans and to secure your approval, as we do not know your whereabouts.*

Secure my approval? Jason wondered. This didn't sound like Abe. Why would his twenty-three-year-old brother be seeking his approval?

*The last we knew, you were on your way to New York. Lacking an address, we were unable to contact you by telegram. Therefore I am reduced to writing this letter and leaving it in the care of Mrs. Beal. If your vow of last September holds up—to return no sooner than a year—you will be home early in the fall and will be reading this letter then.*

*Know that your brothers agonized over the difficult decision I am about to reveal. We discovered that rushing to the Klondike goldfields is a costly endeavor. A complete outfit costs $500 per man, steamer tickets $100 additional per man. Packing services, according to a prospector we were able to interview, will cost an additional $300 per man, making a total of $900.*

*Unfortunately, our funds fall short. We need $1800. We have only $1300, which includes our inheritances from Father and what we have been able to put by since his passing.*

Oh no, Jason thought. They couldn't have. They wouldn't. Surely they didn't.

*The hour grows late and we have so much to do to be ready. Jason, we have presumed upon your good nature and have withdrawn the $500 Father left you. Without the addition of your funds, we would be reduced to packing our outfits—3,500 pounds when combined—on our own backs over the mountains.*

*Know that we consider you a full partner in this Enterprise of the Brothers Hawthorn, though you will be with us in spirit only. A full third of the riches we expect to reap will be yours.*

*Wish us luck! We intend to save all three of us from the life of the "wage slave," as Father described his and our stations in life. We believe that he and you—especially you with your boundless initiative—would wholeheartedly support our*

*endeavors. Write care of the postmaster in Dawson
City, Northwest Territories, Canada. We remain,
as ever,*

> *Fraternally yours,*
> *Abraham Hawthorn*

Jason folded the letter. He bit his lip. All the wind
had gone out of his sails. What in the world was he going
to do now?

## FOUR

At the verge of departure, the *Yakima* gave three boom-ing blasts. Thousands on the dock sent up a resounding cheer, and five hundred Klondikers crowding the rails waved and shouted their brave good-byes.

Jason Hawthorn was aboard the steamer, but he was in no position to wave farewell. He was in hiding inside a canoe down in the ship's cargo hold, where he'd man-aged to slip under a haphazardly lashed oilskin tarp and wedge himself amid a hodgepodge of gear. His right arm had gone painfully to sleep and his face was mashed against one of the metal buckles on his own canvas pack-sack.

Under the tarp, Jason couldn't see a thing, but he heard the mighty blasts of the ship's whistle and the muffled roar from the throng on the dock. Seconds later the ship lurched into motion, and the tumultuous send-off outside was eclipsed by the din from the close-by steam engines and the terror of horses.

For hours he'd winced at their nervous nickers, their snorts and their kicks as they were being loaded. But this, as the engines came to full power, was unbearable. The horses were nearby in the hold, and it sounded as if they were being butchered alive. He thought that surely someone would do something to calm them: crew from the ship, their owners, anyone.

The plight of the horses stirred the sense of dread he'd been feeling during these long hours in the dark into a near panic of his own. His heart felt as if it had broken loose in his chest. He wasn't getting enough breath.

What had he been thinking? He was sailing for Alaska without a ticket, with only the ten dollars Mrs. Beal had given him, a packsack full of clothes and hard bread and cheese, his bedroll, and a book.

He'd bought the book for a dime from a pushcart peddler in New York, and finished it as the train clacked across Montana. It was called *The Seven Seas* and it was written by Rudyard Kipling. He was glad he still had it with him; he wanted to read it a second time. That book was full of adventure—and an adventure was unquestionably what he was having right now. He might be in a bad spot at the moment, but he had to keep his courage up.

Remember, he told himself. You're on your way to Alaska, and you're only three days behind your brothers. *You can catch them*—you're going lighter than they are. And you can get by for a while on ten dollars. That's all you left home with last September.

It was time to escape the canoe. If he didn't move, he'd be so cramped up, he'd never move again.

With all the noise from the engine room and the horses, Jason couldn't tell if there was anyone around. He wriggled out far enough to determine that the canoe had been placed in a corner atop large wooden crates. His vision was blocked by mounds and mounds of Klondike outfits on pallets and contained by rope nets. So many sacks of flour and beans he'd never seen in his life. Here was a strange contraption: a pair of tandem bicycles joined by two bars of iron, which supported a small skiff. Four people were going to pedal a boat over the mountains? Was that possible?

Jason freed his legs, reached silently back for his packsack. He still couldn't see anyone, but as he lowered himself from the crates, he spied someone not forty feet away, standing next to a trunk and opening a jackknife.

In the next moment, the man with the jackknife spotted him.

The fellow was no older than seventeen, Jason realized. Not one of the crew—he was dressed in an expensive wool suit and wore a derby hat. At first the young man had been startled, but now there was a smile playing at his fleshy lips as he folded the jackknife and slid it into his pocket.

With a confident sort of swagger, the fellow was walking toward Jason. He had a round boyish face, almost a baby face, pasty white, with the exception of a fresh scar over his right eye. The son of the ship's owner? Son of the captain? Not a Klondiker, it didn't seem.

Jason gathered up his father's old mackinaw coat, pressed his floppy black hat down on his head, and hefted his packsack over one shoulder. Best not to act afraid, whoever this was.

"Stowaway, eh?" the fellow said, his tone and his features immediately communicating a sense of power, that of the spider to the fly.

Jason didn't say anything. He was trying to get his bearings. The fellow was alone. What was the jackknife for? What was he doing in the hold? A common thief, is that what he was?

"So, what are *you* doing in here?" Jason replied.

"Ah, but *I've* got a ticket. Haven't you heard, anyone who can't show his ticket is subject to removal?"

Jason smiled. "They forgot to tell me that."

"Frank Barker is my name. My friends also call me Kid."

Jason thought about giving a false name. He'd never done it before, and he wasn't going to start now. He was proud of carrying his father's name. "Jason Hawthorn," he said. "So, are you going to turn me in?"

"Not necessarily," Kid Barker replied from the side of his mouth. "Let's get out of here. I'll show you around the ship."

The slight British accent, Jason thought, was only an affectation.

At the door, Barker unlatched a heavy bolt.

"How'd you get in?"

"One of my vast array of skills," the baby face said with a wink. "I'm sure you've got a catalogful yourself. You're a road kid, obviously."

"Yeah, I've been on the road."

Kid Barker poked his head out, said "Hurry" from the corner of his mouth. In a few seconds they were in a dark corridor.

"Will this packsack on my back give me away?" Jason whispered.

"You won't look suspicious," Barker answered,

"unless you act that way. Half the people on this ship lug their things wherever they go. Untrusting souls."

Jason could still hear the horses. He walked down the corridor toward the awful sound.

Kid Barker stayed close on his heels, like a shadow. "You're going the wrong direction."

"Never mind," Jason said. "There's something I have to see." He pushed aside a swinging door, then gasped. There they were, rows upon rows of horses, stacked so closely that it would be impossible for them ever to lie down during the six-day voyage. And here were the ones who had it worst off, these closest to the heat and the clamor of the engine room. He watched for a minute. At every irregular or high-pitched sound amid the overall cacophony, they were thrown into a kicking, rearing, biting, halter-jerking panic.

"How many horses?" Jason wondered, shaking his head in disbelief.

"They say four hundred–some. At least on this ship it's the horses that have it bad, instead of the people. Down in Tacoma, there's a coal ship called the *Islander* that's being converted to passenger service for eight hundred people. We took a look at it. The horse deck is directly above the so-called first-class accommodations. The only thing between is planking, and there's nothing to stop the yellow rivers from those horses from obeying gravity, if you get my drift. That's when we decided on this ship. Now, let's get out of here. The smell is making me sick."

Jason followed Barker above to the crowded top deck and discovered that the *Yakima* had some serious problems of its own. Every ticket, as he heard many a Klondiker angrily explain to the white-jacketed crew members, was supposed to guarantee a separate berth.

It was promised in black and white, right on the ticket. The passengers had been assigned ten to a cabin, but there were only three berths in each cabin, with floor space for two more at best to spread out blankets. "Where do you expect us to sleep?" people were demanding.

The answer always came with a shrug. "Take shifts."

## FIVE

It was dusk and Jason was at the rail, admiring the mountains of Vancouver Island as they neared to the north and west. He could see the lights of Victoria twinkling, and they reminded him of the time his father had taken him and his brothers there on the ferry many years before. It wasn't rough-hewn, like Seattle. Victoria was civilized and stately and British.

"That's not much of an outfit you've got there," his shadow said, twirling the derby hat on his finger. "Going to Dawson City, are you?"

"Planning on it," Jason told Kid Barker.

"On your own, are you?"

Jason thought about mentioning his brothers. Not to this slippery fellow. "That's the shape of it," he said.

"You're not lacking in self-confidence. I like that." Barker leaned closer, lowered his voice. "I'm going to let you in on a little secret. The *real* money in this gold rush is going to be made in Skagway, by businessmen, not in

27

the Klondike by fools digging holes in the ground."

"Maybe we're not reading the same newspapers," Jason said. "I read Skagway's got two buildings."

"That may be true today, but the Skagway I'm talking about is on its way north right now, in the form of lumber and nails, on all these ships. That's what the man I work for says. He's got a vision."

"What kind of work does he do?"

"Business. Some of everything."

Jason wondered if Kid Barker's boss knew about him prowling around in the hold.

"I'm going to tell him about you," Barker said. "He might give you an opportunity."

Jason didn't reply. Kid Barker was leaving; that was all that mattered.

Jason hid his packsack behind some boxes and set off to circle the crowded deck. He ran square into a line of Klondikers extending almost from bow to stern. The line turned a corner and continued down to the next level, and it didn't appear to be moving. All these people were waiting to get into the dining room, he discovered, and they were angry. The dining room seated only twenty-six people.

The stern was crowded with yapping and howling dogs, dogs that were whimpering, and dogs too beaten-looking to make a sound. They were confined in crates scarcely big enough for many of them, and many of them were large dogs: Newfoundlands, Great Danes, mastiffs, wolfhounds, huskies, Saint Bernards, and collies. He overheard one man telling another that he'd bought reindeer to use as his pack animals, but there wasn't room for them on this ship. He'd have to wait in Skagway for them to arrive.

Jason had denied his hunger long enough. He

returned to the spot near the bow where he had stashed his pack, anxious for his bread and cheese.

Kid Barker was there, looking around for him. "There you are, Hawthorn. This is your lucky day! Captain Smith wants you to have supper with us."

"The ship's captain?" Jason asked, starting to panic.

Kid Barker laughed. "No. Captain Jefferson Randolph Smith is my boss. He's the man I told you about."

Jason hesitated. "Line's too long. I think I'll wait until tomorrow."

"We won't have to wait in any line." The Kid gave him a long, meaningful look with a hint of menace in it. "Come on, I insist. It's an opportunity for you. These are the future business leaders of Skagway."

Jason couldn't risk being turned in as a stowaway and getting put off the ship in the middle of nowhere. He had to catch up with his brothers. It would be a dangerous mistake to put more time between him and them.

Kid Barker led him up a flight of stairs, then ducked under a NO ADMITTANCE sign attached to a chain across a hallway. They passed by the cabins of the first officer and the ship's captain. Barker gave three quick raps at a door marked RAINIER SUITE.

A ship's steward in white jacket and trousers opened the door slightly. Through thick cigar smoke, Jason made out four men playing cards in a sumptuous lounge with ornate furniture and green-and-gold scrollwork on the walls.

"Come in," a mellow southern voice called.

Jason didn't know what he was expecting. Here was a group as distinguished as he might ever like to meet, wearing wing collars, diamond stickpins, and polished high-button boots. The dark-bearded, gentlemanly Smith introduced him to the Reverend Charles Bowers,

Old Man Tripp, and Jim Foster, who looked Ethan's age and was disarmingly sincere. They called in supper for him, then went back to their game.

They didn't seem to want anything. The food was good, and Jason couldn't help but feel thankful for the meal.

Well? Kid Barker's expression seemed to say as they were leaving.

"Join us again tomorrow evening," Captain Smith called.

Somehow, it sounded like a command.

Putting the three-hundred-mile barrier of Vancouver Island behind, the *Yakima* steamed into the open ocean. At once, the sea was hilly with wind-driven whitecaps, and the deck began to pitch with a sickeningly monotonous motion.

Within a few hours the ship entered a dark bank of clouds and it began to rain. The rain stayed with them for days, all the way through Canadian waters and into the archipelago of Alaska with its thousand islands.

Coughing and cold, Jason spent two nights on the open decks and one under a tarp with generous Klondikers who'd waved him in. Though he was dressed in his long flannel underwear and a woolen shirt, woolen trousers, wool socks, and his father's plaid mackinaw coat, this was still a penetrating, bone-shivering cold.

He could have been sleeping on a cot in the Rainier Suite all the while, but he'd told Kid Barker that he preferred to sleep in the open, no matter the circumstances, and halfway convinced him it was true. It was important to keep as much of his independence as he could without riling them.

He had to keep coming for dinner, though. Smith had insisted. Had Kid Barker, at the outset, told Captain Smith that Jason was a stowaway?

Without a doubt.

What did Smith want, then? Every evening, Jason showed up like a wet dog from the alley, and they fed him. They weren't saying what they wanted yet, but Jason knew it was coming. Was there any chance they would wait until Skagway?

If they did, he'd be gone before they even noticed.

Contemptuous of the Klondikers, Barker stayed away from the crowds on deck. Jason relished their talk, especially when it came to panning and placers and sluice boxes and "shiny nuggets thick as gravel." In his mind, he was already on a northern creek with his brothers, panning and shoveling and sacking up the gold.

As Jason was leaving the Rainier Suite the fourth evening, Smith beckoned him over and said in his mellow drawl, "Time you started learning the ropes. I've asked the Kid to take care of it tomorrow."

Jason was caught off guard. What was he going to say? What was Smith talking about? The safest thing he could do, he thought, was to stall for time. After tonight, only one more night. He couldn't afford to be put off the ship. The following day they'd be in Skagway.

He nodded, said nothing.

The sleepy-eyed Smith nodded in return, then showed his cards to his companions—a royal flush. The tall, curly-haired young man, "Slim Jim" Foster, exclaimed, "And they call *me* Magic Fingers!"

There'd been no money on the table. The Reverend Charles Bowers, who Smith said was going to open the first church in Skagway, was one of the players. If Smith had cheated, apparently it was all in fun.

Jason left the suite as confused as ever.

In the morning the sun broke through at last and burned the clouds away. Their only vestiges clung to the high peaks. On the deck of the ship, the stampeders' wool clothes steamed vapor into the sunlight and people were excited to be drawing near to the starting line. They gaped at the mountainsides pitching up from the sea, all cloaked with dark timber, and they pointed to the glaciers high above and to waterfalls that plunged in steps thousands of feet to the sea.

Kid Barker appeared on the deck that day and said, "Stick close and learn." Suddenly Barker was among the passengers he disdained, cheerful as a songbird with his British accent. After exchanging pleasantries with a short, well-groomed man and his wife—the woman was especially charmed—Barker said, "No doubt you've heard the warning from C. N. Bliss, the United States Secretary of the Interior."

"No, what is it?" came the anxious reply.

"An official government warning, no less, to the effect that it might already be too late to reach the Klondike before winter. That it would be dangerous even to attempt it."

"Surely no. What do *you* think?"

"I think it all depends on a man's funds. If he can afford to pay for horse packing over the White Pass, or for the Indian packers to carry his outfit over Chilkoot Pass, then it certainly won't be a problem. But if a man has to carry his own outfit on his back in stages, with a boat yet to build and five hundred miles of the Yukon River to descend . . . well, then it can't be done."

There was a hard thump as the Klondiker rapped his wallet in the breast pocket of his mackinaw. "We won't be left behind," the man vowed as he cast a reassuring glance at his dainty wife. "Don't you worry, dear. We'll be hiring those packers. Before you know it, we'll be picking nuggets and shoveling gold. We won't be caught by winter."

"Glad to hear it," Barker said with a smile. "Well, good fellow, Godspeed to you."

Jason didn't know what to think of this encounter, and several others like it, until late that afternoon when crew members passed among the crowd warning of pickpockets. "A man and his wife have lost all their money—a considerable amount. Keep a close watch on your wallets and valuables!"

"You," whispered Jason to Barker. "It was you."

With a smile, Barker said, "I assure you, it wasn't. It's a team effort, Hawthorn. I showed you how my half is played. Fingers even nimbler than mine played the other half."

"You found out who had money and plenty of it, and where they kept it."

"Which is to be your role, once we get to Skagway. You have an honest face—you'll be good at this. There will be hordes coming off the ships, Hawthorn, tens of thousands flooding into Skagway. There are a thousand ways to separate a fool from his money once we know who has it and where he keeps it."

His face flushing, Jason was about to speak. With a raised hand, Barker held him off. "A month or two from now you could be rich beyond your wildest dreams. Isn't that why you wanted to go to Dawson City?"

"I had a father—," Jason replied.

"So?"

"He fought at Gettysburg. He taught me a few things about honor."

Barker started to laugh, then saw that Jason was firm as granite. "You're a fool, Hawthorn," he said, his voice heavy with malice. "You'll regret this."

## SIX

When the three crewmen pulled him aside, Jason had no ticket to show them, no Klondikers on board to name as his companions. After searching his packsack, they patted him down and took the ten dollars Mrs. Beal had given him. He'd been hoarding it for Skagway. Then they walked him down the gangplank at Juneau in the dark. The three never said who had fingered him as a stowaway, yet Jason never wondered for a second.

"Thief!" one of the men snarled as they yanked him into deeper darkness behind a warehouse. Another punched Jason in the stomach, and the wind went out of him. As he buckled, he saw the silhouette of a raised nightstick. Pain broke like a lightning bolt; then the world exploded away and he felt nothing.

Jason came to in the middle of the night, trembling and alone. He put his hand to the back of his head, where the worst of the pain was coming from. His hair was matted with blood and his scalp screamed at the slightest touch. Beyond the docks, lights were twinkling. This was Juneau, he realized, remembering what had happened. He'd failed to make it to Skagway.

He had failed. He had no money, no food, no home to go back to, and his brothers had no notion he was in Alaska and in bad trouble.

His fear flared into anger at his brothers for what they'd done—taken his $500!

But as he pictured their faces, his anger wouldn't stick. He knew they thought they were doing a good thing. Ethan and Abraham believed they were going to make him rich.

Baby-faced Kid Barker came to mind instead, then "Captain" Smith and "Reverend" Bowers and "Slim Jim" Foster and "Old Man" Tripp. Imposters and crooks, all of them. This was their fault.

A few feet away, the dark shape of his packsack caught his eye. At least he hadn't lost everything—he still had some clothes and his pack. And *The Seven Seas*.

Jason reached for the packsack and dragged it under his head, which he lowered gingerly until it came to rest. He slept.

At dawn he was standing at the beach with his pack on his back and his head throbbing, trying to figure out what to do next. Two piers away, a steamer called the *City of Topeka* was loading cargo and chuffing smoke.

Jason's head felt like it was in a vise and the heavyweight champion of the world was battering it with a sledgehammer.

He'd come so close! One more night on the *Yakima* and he would have been there.

Normally he could keep self-pity at bay. But at the

moment, he was too exhausted. Maybe it was time to give up and head back to Seattle. Maybe the *City of Topeka* is heading south, he thought. They might need coal stokers. I can work my way home.

Jason battled his own weariness. Get up off the mat, he finally told himself. You aren't licked yet. You have more staying power than that.

If he could just get to Skagway somehow, without losing much more time, he could rejoin the race, or the fight—whichever it was going to be.

His stomach twisted on itself and clamored for attention.

You've been this hungry before, he told himself. Many times.

Jason looked north along the gravelly beach. At the high-tide line, the blue smoke of a campfire wound its way into the tops of the giant spruces.

An early-morning campfire meant food. It wouldn't be the first time he'd resorted to a handout. He started walking. His eye was drawn to a patch of bright red halfway down the beach, a red-shirted man using a drift-wood log for a backrest.

The man was reading, Jason realized as he got closer. He looked a little over twenty, right around Ethan's age.

The fellow was so engrossed in his book, he was unaware that anyone was approaching. Clearing his throat, Jason stepped up and asked, "What are you reading? Must be pretty good."

Surprised, the young man looked up with deep-set blue-gray eyes that sparkled with intelligence. "*Origin of Species*, by Charles Darwin," he replied. Red Shirt's broad smile owed part of its cheerfulness somehow to a missing tooth.

"Isn't Darwin the one who says we're descended from apes?"

"Yep," Red Shirt said, springing athletically to his feet. He was of average height, only an inch or two taller than Jason, with powerful square shoulders. The fellow stuck out his hand. "Name's Jack."

They shook. "Jason."

"And what if we *are* descended from apes, Jason?" the young man asked with a provocative, playful gleam in his eyes. "How would that suit you?"

Before Jason could answer, the stranger's eyes went to the matted hair toward the back of Jason's head. "Got a bad whack there, looks like."

"Pirates," Jason said with a smile. It was easy to banter with this fellow, Jack.

"Ah . . . did they get your gold?"

"Fortunately, I hadn't gotten it yet."

"You're on your way to the Klondike?"

"I *was*. I'd like to be."

Jack looked toward the pier and Juneau, where Jason had come from. "Where's your outfit, Jason? Your partners?"

"I'm on my own hook," he replied.

"A man after my own heart, but I wouldn't like my chances solo on this trip."

"It's not by design. I'm trying to catch my brothers; they're only a few days in front of me. How far is Skagway? Do you know?"

Jack grinned. "You're closing in on it, my friend. Eighty miles or so. I didn't see you on the *City of Topeka*."

"I was on the *Yakima*. It stopped here last night to take on water for its boilers."

Jack's blue-gray eyes were speculating why Jason had ended up on the beach alone in Juneau. He pushed a tangle of his wavy dark hair back from his forehead and looked north to the campfire. "At least one of my partners is vertical. That's a hopeful sign. You wouldn't be interested in some flapjacks and bacon by any chance?"

"I'd cut off my right foot for breakfast, I don't mind saying."

Jack's open, laughter-loving face was radiant with generosity and the offer of friendship. "Let's walk slow," Jack said. "You got me dying of curiosity on a number of counts. Would you swap me your story in exchange for those flapjacks?"

They started down the beach, Jack pausing to pick up a throwing stone and sail it out toward one of the buoys marking the shipping channel. Jason joined in and it became a friendly contest. In between throws, Jason sketched his story all the way from New York to the nightstick on his head.

At the last, Jack winced. "Could have come out far worse—you might have ended up in Juneau's jail. What happened to you last night brings to mind a month I spent in Buffalo, New York, in the state penitentiary. You look surprised. . . . It was during a year I tramped from California to the East and back. I went to see the falls at Niagara and ended up on the rock pile for vagrancy. They locked me up because I couldn't name a local hotel. . . . It doesn't take much if they're out to get you." As if for emphasis, Jack reached for a stone and heaved a splendid throw that came up barely short of a buoy.

Inspired by the combination of Jack's toss and his

story, Jason put everything he had into his next throw and actually struck the buoy. It rang like a bell.

"Well, I'll be," Jack declared, shaking his head. "I've never been bested at rock throwing in my life. You've got not only distance but accuracy. Where'd you get an arm like that?"

Jason chuckled, disbelieving his own success. "Don't ask me to repeat that. It's from tossing a baseball with my brothers—I've had a lot of practice. You should see my mitt. It looks like a chewed-up scrap of leather that a dog's been hauling around."

They were close enough to camp now that they could smell the bacon frying. Four men were moving around. At Jason's bidding, his new friend went on to tell a little more of his own story. Jack was from Oakland, California. He'd worked in a cannery too—ten cents an hour, twelve hours a day—and a jute mill and a laundry. At seventeen, he was working on a sealing ship in the Arctic. He'd hoboed east after that, then returned to Oakland and the life of a "work beast," as he put it, until the Klondike broke.

Jack had been on fire to go north but had no money. His sister Eliza and her husband, Captain Shepard, had grubstaked him in exchange for helping to get Captain Shepard to the goldfields. Jack's brother-in-law was sixty years old and a veteran of the War Between the States.

On the voyage north, Jack and Captain Shepard had formed a partnership with the three other men on the beach.

"You weren't able to get a ship going all the way to Skagway?" Jason wondered aloud.

"Not one that was leaving soon enough. But last

night we hired the rest of the trip in Indian canoes. We met a party of Tlingits on their way north to work in the packing trade."

Jason was about to ask if there might be room for him in a canoe, but they'd arrived in camp, and four pairs of eyes were on him.

Jack introduced him to his partners and made a joke about Jason helping to lighten the mountain of food they were going to have to carry over the Chilkoot Pass.

Jason remembered that Kid Barker had mentioned the Chilkoot Pass. "Is that a better route than the White Pass?"

"Ten miles shorter," one of the men said curtly. Merritt Sloper didn't look overjoyed about one of his partners inviting a sixth for breakfast.

"Supposed to be an old Indian trail," rasped Captain Shepard, who seemed short of breath. Shepard had a grizzled beard and wore a wide-brimmed Stetson over his silver hair. "The Chilkoot's so steep at the last pitch, they say your chin might overtop your eyebrows if you look up to the summit."

Everyone laughed. Jason thought he heard a good deal of apprehension in the old man's voice about this Chilkoot Pass.

Another partner, a man named Goodman, was pointing south toward the end of the pier. A number of tall-prowed Indian canoes were paddling in their direction.

Eleven canoes, it turned out to be. The Indians kept their streamlined and somewhat fragile dugouts in the shallows and walked ashore, men, women, and children. With no discussion, they headed directly toward the mounded outfits and started shouldering the supplies to the canoes.

In half an hour, everything was loaded. Jack's partners were wading out to the canoes. Jack was last. He
seemed to be eyeing the space that was left, if any.

So was Jason, as best as he could from the beach.
The canoes were heavily loaded.

A steamer passed them by, heading north. Hundreds
of stampeders were waving at them from the decks. A
voice like a foghorn hollered down, "Klondike or bust!"

A second steamship appeared behind the first, and
here came a third. Sloper yelled from his canoe, almost
frantically, "Come on. Let's go!"

Boarding the last dugout, Jack looked inside it for a
moment, then waved Jason forward. "Get in. You need
to catch your brothers!"

## SEVEN

Weeks before, any ship moving up the fjord north of Juneau would have been alone. Suddenly the narrow channel under the towering peaks was streaming with heavy traffic. Anything that could float had been thrown into the trade.

The destination was the dagger tip of the fjord, where the sea met a mountain wall. Two small rivers entered the ocean there within three miles of each other—the Dyea and the Skagway. At the mouth of the Dyea River, civilization consisted of a trading post that for eleven years had served the trickle of prospectors heading up the river canyon, over the Chilkoot Pass, and on to the headwaters of the Yukon River.

The Chilkoot was an ancient "grease trail," a trading route long controlled by the Raven clan of Tlingit Indians from a nearby village. The Tlingits packed their prized fish oil and their blankets straight up over the pass on their backs, then returned with pelts, hides, and copper from the interior. At the time the first prospectors started coming, in the 1870s, the clan still maintained a packing monopoly over the pass, but even before the Klondike erupted in '97, Indians from all up and down the coast had come to take advantage of the increasing demand for packers.

Several miles southeast of the Dyea trading post, at the mouth of the Skagway River, a retired steamboat captain and his family had been waiting ten years for the boom to arrive. The canny William Moore was convinced that it was only a matter of time before a gold rush would send tens of thousands streaming into the Yukon. And he was ready.

Moore believed that a second, less-used Indian trail—one he named White Pass—would offer a far more practical route to the goldfields than the rugged Chilkoot. At forty-five miles, the White Pass route was ten miles longer but six hundred feet lower. Most importantly, horses could be put to use over White Pass. Until horses learned to fly, one would never reach the summit of the stupendously steep Chilkoot. Moore had homesteaded the mouth of the Skagway River, banking on his vision that a town would rise there one day—and he would own all the land.

The first gold-rush steamer arrived on Moore's doorstep July 26, 1897. Within a week, a flotilla plugged the bay. None of the ships could approach closer than a mile to either Skagway or Dyea. The last mile was all shallows and muddy tidal flats that were exposed or submerged, depending on the tides, which fluctuated thirty feet. Klondikers had to lower or throw down their outfits onto clumsy flat-bottomed scows, which ferried the supplies to the beach. There, everything was dumped onto the muddy gravel, even if the tide was rising. Men by the hundreds labored to save their outfits from the sea.

It was into this pandemonium that eleven Indian canoes threaded their way shoreward among the steamers anchored off of Dyea. Jason recognized the *Yakima* even before he saw its name. At close range he saw the unlucky horses from the hold being dropped one at a time, kicking and terrified, from a big wooden box into the sea. After all they'd endured, now they had to thrash their way onshore, and some of them were drowning right before his eyes.

Another ship that had just arrived was in the heat of unloading. Steamer trunks dropped onto the scows below were bursting open, men were cursing, dogs and goats were being thrown into the sea to swim for shore.

Even from a distance, Jason could see that the beach was swarming with people moving gear. Some of the goods were going onto horse-drawn freight wagons, but most Klondikers were shouldering their own supplies from the scows to the high-tide line. It reminded Jason of the frenzy inside an anthill busted open with a boot. But what looked like ants lugging their oval white eggs helter-skelter were Klondikers rescuing sacks of flour and beans.

It started raining.

Beyond the beach, the mouth of the narrow river valley was choked with canvas wall tents. Smoke from dozens of campfires met the lowering clouds.

The Indians paddled the eleven canoes into the mouth of the Dyea River. Beyond the tents, there was a single log cabin—a trading post. "Let's not stop," Sloper shouted back from the lead canoe. "Let's see how far we can get up the river today."

"I'm all for it!" Jack shouted back. "Hey, look at the salmon!"

The stream was thick with them—bright red, with greenish heads.

Up ahead, the river was shallowing. The packers got out of the canoes and started wading, pulling the canoes after them on ropes.

Jason was fretting. Which way had his brothers gone, Dyea and the Chilkoot Pass, or Skagway and White Pass? He was going to have to choose.

Jack climbed out of the canoe and started wading in his rubber boots. Jason's boots were leather. The water was ice-cold!

The rain came harder. Men were pulling out their rain slickers. Jason didn't have one. You've been wet before, he told himself. Captain Shepard was coughing, and looking even older than his sixty years.

Jason didn't like the sound of this Chilkoot Pass—straight up at the end. "How much do the packers charge over the Chilkoot?" he asked Jack.

"Thirty cents a pound. We're just sticking with them as far as they can get the canoes up the river. Maybe Thompson can pay, but the rest of us can't. That'd be $600 for one man's outfit!"

"You're going to hump it over yourself?"

"That's my plan."

It made Jason wonder what his brothers had done with their $600 of packing money. "Any idea what horse packing costs over on White Pass?"

"Can't say."

He couldn't be asking Jack to guess which way his brothers had gone.

His brothers wouldn't have liked the sound of this straight-up Chilkoot any more than he did. Horses could go faster. He'd done some cowboying last fall in Wyoming—helped an old man pack a sheep camp out of the mountains. A packhorse carrying two hundred pounds could cover forty miles in a couple of days. That's what would make sense to his brothers. Maybe they were still over in Skagway, trying to hire horses!

Jason reached into the canoe and pulled out his pack. "I'm going to try White Pass," he told Jack.

Jack stopped wading and clapped him on the shoulder. "Good luck to you, Jason! Hope you find your Golden Fleece!"

Jason laughed. "I wouldn't be disappointed if my gold was the hard, shiny kind instead of a gold sheepskin."

They shook hands. "Thank you," Jason said. "You really helped me out. Hope we meet again—maybe in Dawson City, when both of us have struck it rich. What's your last name, so I can ask after you?"

"London."

Jason turned and waded downstream, back to the confusion at the beach. More Indian canoes were starting up the river. He heard someone say that the Dyea River was navigable for five miles upstream. He was happy about that for Jack London—fewer miles to have to lug his ton of gear on his own back.

It was three miles over to Skagway, and it couldn't be walked. Fortunately there were scows plying back and forth, and he was able to pile onto one without forking over a dollar he didn't have. The walrus-mustached operator wasn't paying any attention. In the chaos of all these shouting people, the mud and the rain and the dogs shaking themselves in his face, the scow pilot looked like Alaska's version of Charon, sentenced to ferry people across the river to hell.

Skagway's beach was like Dyea's, only worse: piles of gear, stacks of hay and lumber, horses by the hundreds wandering untethered and knocking things over, dogs being whipped, men setting up tents and cooking meals on their Klondike stoves. A hundred yards out on the naked tidal flats, a strange contraption was mired in the mud amid heaps of provisions that had been lost to salt water. It was the two tandem bicycles spanned by the iron bars he'd seen in the *Yakima*'s hold. The bicycles hadn't even made it onto the beach.

Jason hopped and stepped through the black muck of Skagway's main street—BROADWAY, a flimsy sign proclaimed. The town was another anthill of activity, with saws and hammers going on all sides and a slowly moving stream of rushers and freight wagons choking the muddy street. Some Klondikers were leading packed horses and some were dragging dogs harnessed to sleds heaped high with gear. The procession passed through a line of thrown-together shacks and the frames of two- and even three-story hotels under construction. Jason counted four saloons, a drugstore in a tent, a blacksmith advertising five dollars a shoe, a restaurant with MEALS— $3 written across the seat of a hanging pair of ragged trousers. Tent sites were being offered at ten dollars apiece.

Jason waited in front of two different packing offices, hoping to ask if and when his brothers had hired their services. But there were so many men trying to get inside, he finally gave up and kept walking. Another two blocks and Broadway ran smack into someone's house, a tidy two-story frame structure that had obviously been there for a number of years.

There was a huge commotion under way. One old man armed with a crowbar was trying to stand off a hun-

dred. They'd come to move his house out of the way of
the street, and he'd already ripped a leg off a fellow's
trousers while defending his property. The old man kept
claiming that every bit of the town was being illegally
erected on his property, but he was met by nothing but
jeers.

"I'm Captain William Moore," he cried, "and all of
you are trespassing! All this ground you're standing on
belongs to *me.*"

Jason kept moving, following the Klondikers who
were streaming around the old man's house and out of
town. He didn't care if he never laid eyes on Skagway
again.

It would be dark in a couple of hours. He had to find
something to eat and somewhere to sleep. He passed a
dozen "restaurants" along the wagon road leading out of
town—stampeders cooking at their Klondike stoves and
selling meals. Ahead, the wagon road was about to make
its first crossing of the Skagway River. He was hoping
there'd be salmon running in that river.

And there were.

Jason wasn't the only one with the idea. Like bears,
men were standing in the river and fishing out salmon—
some with their hands, some with spears whittled from
the alders along the shore.

In a little while Jason had a salmon. He had a salmon
and a jackknife and he had matches in a waterproof
match safe. The night before, he'd watched how the
Indians spread their salmon open with whittled sticks
and roasted them upright beside the campfire. He did
the same and ate his fill, then went looking for berries.
They were plentiful. Salmon and berries: For the time
being, he was living the life of an Alaskan bear.

It was drizzling again. Jason got back on the wagon

road and started walking. He was going to find a stand of spruces thick enough to keep the rain off while he was sleeping. He needed to keep his bedroll dry.

There was a wall tent ahead that had been erected beside the road. He saw a sign and thought it might be advertising another restaurant. But there was a bad stink in the air, like carrion. As he drew closer, he realized to his horror that the sign had been placed at the foot of a pole where a man had been tied up, then shot repeatedly. The sign by the corpse said THIEF.

All the while the people went streaming by. Like the rest, he kept on going.

## EIGHT

In the morning Jason rejoined the river of humanity streaming along the wagon road. He made good time as the road stayed to the valley floor, but after three miles the valley pinched to a close against the rising mountains and the wagon road came to an abrupt end. At the river crossing, freight wagons were unloading and Klondikers by the hundreds were transferring their gear to horseback.

As it began to rain again, Jason stopped for a minute and surveyed the confusion. A few of the horses looked all right, but most were in deplorable condition. From his own horse-packing experience in Wyoming, it was apparent that most of the stampeders had never worked with a horse in their lives. It pained him to see men putting pack saddles on backward, some not even using saddle blankets. Worse than that, some men were so angry, they were terrifying the horses with curses and even whips.

51

Suddenly it occurred to Jason that he was looking at his meal ticket, his big opportunity. These *horses*, he thought. These horses can feed me until I catch up to my brothers!

He watched for a while longer, then picked out a pair of men struggling in frustration. At least these two weren't taking it out on the horses.

Jason stepped up, introduced himself, then told the men he'd packed horses. He offered to wrangle their horses for meals and ten dollars a day, paid daily. It was an outrageous amount, but prices were beyond belief up here. Without hesitation, the two men accepted his offer. One joked that when they'd bought these animals in Seattle, they hadn't known one end of a horse from the other. Their names were Robinson and Bailey. They were clerks from Philadelphia who'd left jobs and families behind to go for broke on the rush.

Jason found the men good-natured. His own spirits soared now that he knew he'd get fed and be earning good money. Together they led the horses across the river and joined the slow line of stampeders climbing the first hill.

The mood soon turned grim as forward progress slowed to a crawl. It was walk a minute, wait a minute. Jason and Bailey were leading six packhorses apiece while Robinson dragged their sled, which couldn't handle much weight on the dirt and mud. Everyone in line was half-frantic to be on the other side of the pass and building boats. People were worrying about winter catching them before they could make it to Dawson City. "Must be some bottleneck up ahead," Bailey fretted. "Once we're past it we'll be okay."

It kept raining. When wasn't it raining in Alaska? One of the many times the line stopped altogether, Jason found himself standing right next to a dead horse that lay by the side of the trail. He tried not to look into the empty eye sockets and struggled to block out the stench from its belly, ripped open by the birds. He was afraid he was going to be sick.

Jason felt his earlier optimism draining away. He was never going to catch his brothers at this rate. Progress had become so agonizingly slow, it was close to midnight before they put the trail's first obstacle, Devil's Hill, behind them. They set up the canvas wall tent in the lingering twilight. Robinson and Bailey unlashed the fat little sheet-iron stove from the sled, set up a few sections of flue, and cooked supper. Jason went out in the woods and cut spruce boughs for bedding. It was raining hard, and rivulets poured through the tent.

Exhausted as he was, Jason couldn't sleep. His bedding was soaked and the cut end of a spruce branch was jabbing him in the back.

After only three or four hours, they were up and moving again in the long twilight preceding dawn. The trail was already choked with stampeders. Clouds shrouded the mountainsides, making it impossible to see the chalk-white peaks. It rained or it drizzled. The weight of all the horses ahead had churned the soggy trail into a quagmire.

The three of them almost never spoke now. They had become like the horses, struggling in the muck, spouting vapor jets in the rain, reduced to the brute essentials of breathing and moving forward when possible. Delays were frequent and endless. Mostly they waited, with no more consciousness than the tail end of a snake, not knowing what the front of the line was seeing or doing or when it might advance again, and them with it.

Part of the problem, Jason realized, was traffic moving down the trail, back toward Skagway. Some were retreating stampeders, who'd lost too many horses and too much gear, or the will to keep going. Some were professional packers returning on horseback from Lake Bennett at the end of the trail. "I'm looking for my brothers, Abe and Ethan Hawthorn," Jason told wranglers heading back to Skagway. "Did you pack them over the pass?"

"Nope," came the reply every time, "not us."

As the days ran together, the waiting grew worse. All along the line, the gaunt horses stood in the trail, nose-to-tail under their crushing two- and three-hundred-pound loads. No one could afford the mercy of unpacking them during the delays. The serpent might start to move again.

Some Klondikers weren't even bothering to unpack their horses at night. Jason could imagine all too well the agony of the mute animals all around him. Most were half-starved to begin with, and there was virtually no grass under the dense forest. Rare was the party that was packing any hay. His wasn't.

Every mile there were more dead horses along the trail, and from all sides came the croaking of ravens.

The ravens always took the eyes first.

Half an hour rarely went by without a pistol shot from ahead or behind. The third morning, Bailey brought out his own pistol when one of their horses couldn't rise. The blast tore a hole in Jason's sense of fair play. He was part of this, he knew, coaxing and dragging these poor creatures to their death. He felt like an accomplice in a crime.

"That's Porcupine Hill," he heard somebody say. He looked up to see a jumble of boulders above, gigantic boulders, with horses squeezing between. It took an excruciatingly slow hour to reach those boulders. When they did, a horse was down in the trail not far ahead and neighing in torment. "Broken leg," came the report down the line. "Turned its leg in a crevice." Jason saw the butt end of an ax raised high in the air. He turned away, numb and shivering in the drizzle. The dull, bone-crushing thud came like a pronouncement of doom.

It would have taken time and effort to remove the carcass from that spot between the boulders. Men, women, and animals resumed the march right over the horse's body.

Jason had lost all sense of time. As best he could recall, they'd been under way for six days. It had all run together, connected by shouts and curses and the cloying stench of death. Far below, under the cliffs, the dead horses lay in heaps. They lay everywhere along the sides of the trail, hundreds and hundreds of them. White Pass had gotten a new name—everyone was call-ing it the Dead Horse Trail.

Jason was ashamed and sick at heart. Still, the night-mare went on. More and more people were retreating down the trail in the muck. A man sat along the side of the trail stone-cold dead, shot through the back. Another man, enraged with his ox, which had become mired in the mud, was burning its belly with a torch. Still the ox couldn't free itself, only bellow in pain. Jason watched a packhorse walk right off the edge of a cliff—a suicide? Grown men sobbed their hearts out in despair.

And now they were looking at a thousand-foot climb in the rain up streaming rivers of mud. For two hours they waited for their turn to start up it. "Couldn't we camp right here?" Bailey asked.

Robinson coughed and spat. "No level ground."

All around them people were retreating. Some were admitting they were beaten. Others were going to try the Chilkoot.

With so many trying to move in opposite directions, it was chaos. "We've covered only fourteen miles," Bailey said to his partner. "Fourteen miles in a week."

"I've seen enough," Robinson said. "I'm done. Let's go home."

Jason helped them turn their horses around, then watched them go. He shouldered his packsack. His brothers were in front of him, not behind. He had sixty dollars in his pocket; he could buy meals from stampeders now if only he could keep moving forward.

A few minutes later he tried to skirt a bad bottleneck in the trail. A man with crazed bloodshot eyes drew his pistol. "You do that and I'll shoot you dead."

It was obvious he would.

Jason stayed put. What was he going to do?

Immobilized, he sat along the trail in the drizzle, coughed and shivered. He didn't know how much more cold and wet and misery he could stand. Two men on horseback were picking their way down the trail. These two didn't have the stamp of defeat on them. Professional packers, he guessed.

"Did you pack for the Hawthorn brothers, by any chance?"

The first man nodded. "Abe and Ethan Hawthorn."

Jason was thunderstruck. "When did they get to Lake Bennett?"

"Four days ago."

"Can I catch them before they get a boat built?"

"Doubtful. It's like this all the way. Your brothers were lucky to be on the front end, before all this happened."

"What if I try the Chilkoot?"

"If you travel light, you might catch them. The Chilkoot's mostly rock, not slime like this."

"Thanks. Thanks a lot."

With no hesitation, Jason shouldered his pack and started downhill. People were letting him around, as long as he was retreating. Finally he could fly, put this nightmare behind him.

Descending Porcupine Hill, he passed through a slot between two boulders. On one side of the trail was a horse's head, on the other its hind legs. This, he realized, was the horse he'd seen killed with the ax blow to the head. This was all that remained; the rest had been ground into the mud.

A few minutes later, where a stream plunged across the trail, he came across a man in an utter rage, a burly man with red suspenders who seemed to be holding one of his dogs underwater. That's exactly what he was doing—he was drowning the dog!

Jason's eyes went to the bodies of three dead dogs among the rocks downstream. In the cursing, roaring height of passion, the man was drowning every one of his dogs!

The human serpent, meanwhile, was passing by with only mild curiosity.

Jason couldn't pass by. Mouth agape, he stepped away from the line. The dog in the madman's huge hands was dead now; it floated downstream toward the others. With a bearlike roar, the man turned to unbuckle his fifth and last dog from the tug line. It was a black-and-white husky, a big male, big enough that it should have been trying to resist.

Jason was trembling. His face was flushing hot, his fists clenching and unclenching helplessly.

Like the horses on the trail, the dog seemed to rec-
ognize its fate, and had accepted it. The husky simply lay
on its side and rolled its eyes away from the spectacle of
the man who'd lost his reason. The man with the red
suspenders grabbed up the dog by its harness and
plunged its head and shoulders under the water, pinning
the husky with his knee.

Jason could stand no more. He'd seen too much cru-
elty, had played his part in it. No matter the conse-
quences, he had to do something. He threw his pack to
the ground and waded into the creek hollering, all out of
control. Seizing the man by his collar and an elbow,
Jason spun him around and screamed "No! No!" into his
face.

The huge man rose menacingly over Jason, and as
he rose he released the dog. Eyes blazing like burning
coals, he pulled out a pistol, put it to the side of Jason's
head, and cocked it.

"If you don't want him," Jason pleaded, "leave him
be. I'll take him!"

The man pushed him away, then looked at him
crazily. A weird smile began to play at his cracked lips.
"Take him, then. He's yours!"

The dog drowner started laughing maniacally. "He
won't pull! Two hundred dollars and he won't pull. Take
him!"

Jason tugged at the dog's harness. "Let's go," he said
to the animal.

His eyes met the eyes of the dog, and Jason recognized a flicker of hope in their amber depths. "Come
with me," Jason said. The husky got to its feet and
waded tentatively out of the stream, keeping a wary eye
on its tormenter. Jason grabbed up his packsack and
started walking down the trail. "Come on," he encour-

aged, beckoning. The husky came with him, and neither looked back.

A few moments later there came an explosive pistol shot. Jason jerked his head around, wondering if he was being shot at. The big man had blown his brains out.

## *NINE*

In little more than a week, Skagway had grown dramatically. The buildings along Broadway were virtually completed.

Jason couldn't resist the temptation to eat at a restaurant, even if a meal cost twelve times what it would have in Seattle. At a thrown-together establishment called the Midas Café, he ordered a New York steak and handed over three dollars.

As he took his first bite, he detected a slight rancid odor. But then he decided that the odor was coming from him. He and his clothes were full of the scent of dead horses.

As Jason ate he listened to the subdued conversation of two men at the table behind him. There was a secretive tone to their voices that made him strain to hear what they were saying. They'd been in Skagway a week, he understood that much, trying to arrange to have their outfits packed over White Pass—the Dead Horse Trail. "I believe we've landed in hell," one of them said.

"A shooting every night!"

"It's not just the gamblers. Anyone you do business with might be a swindler. There's even one posing as a preacher. Some of their victims have barely stepped off the ships."

"Going bust on the trail is one thing, but being cheated out of your funds before you even set out is another. Seen all the FOR SALE signs down by the water—people selling their outfits off cheap?"

"Everything from fur hats to Winchesters. People just trying to raise enough money to get back to Seattle. And the law—they do nothing."

Suddenly the other voice went down to a bare whisper. "People are saying that the marshal is working for the boss of Skagway. If you report a crime, you might be digging your own grave."

"So, who *is* the boss of Skagway?"

"That southerner who poses as a philanthropist—Jeff Smith."

Captain Jefferson Randolph Smith, Jason almost said aloud. He fought the impulse to turn around and tell those two men about his own encounter with Smith and his bunch. Instead, he chewed slowly, listened intently, said nothing.

"They say Smith gives people the fare home, sometimes, out of his own pocket."

"After his men have cheated or robbed them!"

"There'll be many a dry eye at his funeral."

"I heard it whispered today, who he really is. . . ."

"What do you mean?"

There was a pause. "I heard tell he's a famous con man from the mining camps in Colorado by the name of

Soapy Smith. Didn't even bother to change his name.
Brought some of his accomplices with him and recruits
others every day. They're everywhere!"

"All I know is, we better get out of here while we still
can. Better try the Chilkoot, don't you think?"

Jason had only a small piece of his steak left. He dangled the meat above the big husky at his feet. The dog
sniffed it, took it gingerly, gummed it, then dropped it to
the floor uneaten.

"Thought you were hungry," Jason said. "You'd pre-
fer fish? I'll try to find you some. What do you say we go
looking for packsacks for you? Would you carry for me,
over the Chilkoot?"

The dog's amber eyes, all the while he spoke,
remained locked on his.

"You'll think about it? Good, let's go!"

At the foot of Broadway, Jason paused to take in the
raw, bustling drama. There were more ships offshore
than before, more arrivals streaming onto the beach,
more mountains of gear, more dogs and horses, more
confusion. As he stood there, shouts erupted in front of
the first building on the street, a telegraph office he
didn't remember from before.

"Come out of there!" a man in the middle of the
street demanded indignantly. He was waving a telegram
in the air as a boy of no more than ten clung to his side,
looking fearfully at the people gathering around.
"Father," the boy pleaded.

"Come out and show the good people your telegraph
lines!" his father raged. "Where are the lines? Where are
the poles? This answer from my wife in Sacramento—
it's a phony! I didn't come all this way to be cheated! Pay
once to send your telegram, pay a second time to receive

the so-called reply. I may have just got here only a few hours ago, but I wasn't born yesterday. Show me the telegraph wires!"

Someone was coming out of the office, scowling. It was Kid Barker!

Kid Barker, with his puffy childlike face, put his hands on his hips and nodded to several men standing at the edge of the crowd. Jason saw one of them slip a badge out of his pocket and pin it to his vest. Seconds later, the protesting newcomer was hustled away by the elbows. The crowd murmured at the sight of the man being led away, with his son crying and running to catch up.

The boy's father resisted suddenly, shook loose of the two men who had him by the arms. Jason saw the flash of a nightstick, heard the whack on the man's head, saw the blood stream down the side of his face. Jason glanced back for only the briefest moment at Kid Barker, who was watching from a safe distance with a smug grin on his face. Jason longed for the opportunity to turn the tables on him, but he didn't know how it could be done.

Jason turned quickly away. He couldn't afford to be recognized. Everyone on the street melted away. It was over.

At the beach, amid the FOR SALE signs, Jason found a pair of dog panniers made of canvas and large enough to match the husky's great size. At bargain prices, he bought five pounds of dried fruit and five pounds of jerky, along with a dozen yeast cakes, and began to load up the dog's packsacks and his own for his sprint over Chilkoot Pass.

Then he set about looking for winter clothes. He

wanted to be prepared for the cold when he joined up with his brothers; there was no telling what might be available in Dawson City. He bought three pairs of wool-lined moose-hide mittens, a beaver hat with fold-down earflaps, a heavy wool sweater, overalls, two thick wool blankets to replace his ruined bedroll, wool socks, a splendid pair of sealskin mukluks for winter boots, and a suit of waterproof oilskin to wear over his father's mackinaw and his wool trousers.

All of a sudden Jason felt a twinge in his gut, sharp like the twist of a knife. He took a deep breath. It passed and was immediately replaced by a dull ache, like he'd swallowed gunpowder.

He willed himself to concentrate on what still needed to be done. He bought a tarp and some rope, so he'd be able to sleep dry. There was the dog to think about too now. The big husky would need dried salmon and plenty of it. Jason had seen a man on the Dead Horse Trail with a whole bale of it, the kind the Indians dried in two long strips connected by the tail. He asked around, found an old woman who told him it was for sale at the trading post in Dyea.

He packed the panniers that he hoped the husky would carry for him, arranging a blanket inside of each so that nothing would jab the dog in the sides. They'd head over to Dyea next.

"I need a name for you," Jason said aloud. "I had a dog once, a long time ago . . . not for very long—a puppy, that's all he was."

He was about to say the name of that long-lost dog out loud. But he had never allowed himself that in all these years. It was a sore spot, a wound that had never healed.

When he finished packing the panniers, they were bulging. He lifted them by the yoke, guessed their combined weight at forty pounds.

Jason talked gently to the dog as he lowered the yoke onto the little saddle blanket he'd placed along the husky's back. To his surprise, the dog stood perfectly still, even gave his hand a quick lick. Jason whispered, "I knew you'd carry for me."

He walked a little with the dog, who seemed unbothered by the bulky panniers. Jason's new companion stayed close to his side. The husky's face, looking up, was so expressive: black above, white below, just like his entire body. Those amber eyes had a lot of gold in them.

Jason petted the husky across the wide crown of his head. The dog nuzzled him affectionately and wagged his great tail, which he carried curved up over his back.

"You were someone's pet, weren't you? Someone's best friend? We can be that too."

Jason stooped to fasten the panniers to the dog's harness. His stomach was cramping badly now, and he was breaking out in a sweat. I really am sick, he thought. Something I ate?

The New York steak, he realized. It really *had* gone bad. For a second he even wondered if it could have been rotten horse flesh he'd eaten, and immediately there seemed little doubt. Welcome to Skagway!

No wonder the husky wouldn't touch it.

Got to keep going, he told himself. It was already midafternoon and he still had to find a scow that would take him across to Dyea, but suddenly he collapsed in agony.

In the middle of the human anthill, he lay writhing like a snake with its head cut off. The pain reached a crescendo, and then his mind switched off like an electric light. He knew nothing more.

He didn't know where he was or how much time had passed. He was too sick to know *who* he was. That he hurt, that he was in a fog of pain, was all he knew.

Two faces kept coming and going in the fog, looking down at him. He had no idea who they belonged to.

One was the face of a man with an enormous gray beard.

The other was the face of a girl, a girl with wavy black hair.

Their faces and their voices came and went in the fog, but he couldn't place them.

There was a third face too, the black-and-white face of a sled dog, which would appear and disappear.

The face of the dog floating in his delirium suddenly melted into the face of a puppy, a black-and-white mutt with floppy ears. It was running toward him.

He would struggle to rise, but the man or the girl would hold him back and tell him to stay where he was. He had no idea where he was or what was happening. "Everything's going to be all right," the girl kept saying, but it wasn't. The little puppy was about to be crushed under the wheels of a wagon. His brothers could see it too, but they were powerless to prevent it. "King!" Jason shouted at the top of his lungs. "King, stop! King, King!"

Then he was standing by an open grave, watching his father's casket sink down into the ground. His oldest brother, Abraham, always so strong, was shaking like a leaf. Ethan, who always had a joke to tell, was bawling like a small child.

Jason looked straight down into the grave. It was a mile deep. It had no bottom at all.

"Here," Abraham said, shoving the puppy into his hands. "Take this dog and give it a name and take good care of it. Everything will be all right."

Whenever the fog thinned, Jason was aware of the girl with hair black as a raven's wing or the man with the enormous gray beard putting a moist towel to his forehead. They propped him up. They made him take sips of water from a glass.

When the fog at last was gone and he remembered who he was, he found himself in a strange room. The girl from the dream was sitting by his bed.

She had black hair and hazel eyes, a couple of freckles on her nose, and he had no idea who she was.

## TEN

"You're going to live after all," the raven-haired girl told him.

He groaned.

The husky stood up beside the bed, nuzzled Jason's hand, and yawned. Jason stroked the black fur crowning the dog's head, remembered him from the dream, and realized that some of what he'd dreamed had been no dream at all. This was the dog from the Dead Horse Trail. "Am I still in Skagway?" he asked.

"Yes, and it's the most dreadful place on earth. We can't wait to get out of here. Who's King? You kept calling the name King. Is that the name of your dog here?"

Jason remembered the puppy from his dream, the dog he'd never gotten over all this time. His brothers had wanted to replace it with another, but he wouldn't let them. Losing it had hurt too much.

68

He was about to tell her that King was not the husky's name.

Then he looked again into the clear eyes of this dog who had awaited death with such calm.

"Yes," he answered. "That's his name. King."

"How about *your* name?" the girl asked.

"Jason. Jason Hawthorn."

She thought about his name, but not for long. "I like that," she announced. "The thorny part isn't necessarily a bad thing. It could be a good thing. Jason is perfect."

What was she talking about? "Who are you?" he asked.

"I'm Jamie Dunavant."

"Jamie?"

"That's right. I'm fourteen years old. My father is Homer Dunavant, and we're on our way to Dawson City."

He sat up straighter. The girl reached for a cushion and propped it behind his back. He was struggling to remember how he had gotten here to this room, but he couldn't.

Jamie seemed to read his mind, and explained. "My father carried you here. We weren't planning to stay overnight in Skagway, but then we came across you. You were *real* sick. My father wanted to stay with you till you got better, but then he got restless and went out and started playing the shell game.

"Father's a poet, and a good one, too. But he has one weakness—he loves to gamble. And guess what? He lost some of our money. There's so many crooks around here, an honest man is like a grasshopper in a yard full of chickens. My father insists that the eye is faster than the hand, and he does win sometimes, but whenever the stakes are high, he loses. There's got to be a trick to it. He's already lost a hundred dollars. Imagine, a hundred dollars! I'm afraid he's out there right now trying to win it back. I'll be happy to get over the Chilkoot and into the jurisdiction of the Yellow Legs."

Jason was trying hard to make sense of all this.

The girl went to the window and looked anxiously up and down the street. "It sure wasn't like this where I'm from."

"Where *are* you from?"

"Swift Water . . . ," she replied absently as she kept her eye out for her father, ". . . west of Moose Jaw and east of Medicine Hat."

"Oh," Jason said uncertainly.

"South of Saskatoon," she explained.

"Montana? North Dakota?"

She wheeled around when she realized how confused he was. "Saskatchewan," she declared. "Saskatchewan, Canada. My father and I are Canadians. We caught the Klondicitis bad, sold the farm, took the Canadian Pacific west to Vancouver and sailed from there. We were headed for Dyea and the Chilkoot Pass, but everyone from our ship got dumped here in Skagway."

"Lucky for me," Jason said. "Who are those Yellow Legs you were talking about, the ones on the other side of the Chilkoot?"

"Oh, them. The Northwest Mounted Police. The Mounties. They have yellow stripes down the sides of their trousers."

In the morning Jason was recovered enough to board a scow for Dyea along with Jamie and her father. On the ride across the tip of the bay, Homer Dunavant was scribbling lines in a notebook. The poet's beard was big enough for birds to nest in.

"Does he sell his poems?" Jason asked the girl.

"Oh, no, but they're good enough. He won't even recite them to people. Too modest."

Jason peeked over the poet's shoulder. The title of the poem was "Lift Up Your Eyes." As the poet wrote each new line, he would look up to the snow-clad peaks. For inspiration, Jason guessed.

"I'll tell you the beginning of one he wrote yesterday," Jamie whispered. "I know it by heart. Listen:

*"Oh, they scratches the earth and it tumbles out,*
*More than your hands can hold,*
*For the hills above and plains beneath*
*Are cracking and busting with gold.*

"How do you like it, Jason?"

"It makes me want to get up there and start digging."

He didn't know what to make of this girl, except that he knew he liked her. Unguarded as a baby colt, she always looked him straight in the eye, and burst out with her enthusiasms. She was different from any girl he'd met, a bright new star in the sky.

When it came to practical matters, Jason couldn't help wondering about these two Canadians. Their things, which he'd helped to load on the scow, consisted of a sleek eighteen-foot canoe and no more than a five-hundred-pound outfit from food to gold pan. It seemed like the poet and his daughter stood only a slightly better chance of reaching the Klondike than the people he'd read about in the Minnesota newspaper who'd announced they were going to go by balloon. But he wasn't going to say it.

He did say, "You sure are going light."

"Fast and light," Jamie replied. "That's Father's strategy. We still have enough funds to pay the Indians to pack our canoe and outfit over to the other side. It's all we have left from selling the farm, less what Father donated to the criminals in Skagway."

She added in a whisper, "We only got a thousand dollars for the farm. We have six hundred left."

"But how will you eat this winter?"

"Father's Winchester will take care of that. He never really was a farmer, you see—we just came out of the North a few years ago, when he got the daft notion that I needed 'civilizing,' as he called it. Before that he worked for Hudson's Bay Company his whole life, trapping and trading. I grew up at Fort Chipewyan on Lake Athabaska, in the bush."

"In a bush, did you say? Excuse me—"

"*The* bush, silly. In the *wilderness*. There's moose, caribou, and mountain sheep in the Yukon country where we're headed—we'll be fine. We can make dry meat, pick berries and make pemmican, gather rose hips for tea. You should do that too, you know—a cup of rose hip tea once a week through the winter and you won't get scurvy."

"What about the Yukon River? Can a canoe handle it?"

"This Peterborough we have is the best canoe in the world! Father says there's no more than five miles of rapids in the whole journey. A beginner could paddle the rest of it in a canoe just fine—and we're not beginners!"

"That Mountie post, wherever it is—aren't you worried about it?"

"It's past Lake Bennett, at the foot of Tagish Lake.

But we won't have to pay a customs duty like you will, because we bought everything in Canada."

"What I was trying to get at is the food requirement. . . . Isn't it seven hundred pounds per person? Will the Mounties let you through with no more than you can carry in the canoe?"

"They'd better. . . . We're Canadian citizens! With my father's experience in the North, he has no doubt he can convince them we'll do fine. All the Yellow Legs care about is that you're not going to go up there and die. It's only a three-week paddle to Dawson City. We'll be there well before freeze-up."

Jason couldn't help but grin. It made him feel good just listening to Jamie, so filled with confidence, so proud of her father and what they were attempting together.

When they reached Dyea, the beach was swarming with the arrival of eight hundred Klondikers from the *Islander* offshore, the converted coal carrier Kid Barker had told him about. The horses, he remembered, were quartered above the first-class berths. He thought better of telling Jamie about those yellow rivers.

He helped his Canadian friends load their canoe. Then Jamie paddled it a short way up the Dyea River, past the melee of horse-drawn freight wagons and Klondikers on foot shuttling their goods to safety above the high-tide line. She would wait there while her father arranged for packers at the Indian huts just beyond the trading post. Jason called his thank-yous and good-byes to both of them, hesitant to turn away. It didn't seem right that he'd never see them again. She was pretty, darn it, in addition to being friendly and brimful of spunk.

With King at his side, Jason finally turned and waded off through the crowd. At the trading post he stood in line to buy a bale of dried salmon for the husky. As he paid, the clerk handed him, without explanation, a map of the trail over Chilkoot Pass, and a second one of the Yukon River to Dawson City. "How long would it take two men to build a boat from timber?" Jason inquired.

"Been done in two weeks," the clerk said impatiently. "That was in the days before all this, though, by men who knew what they were doing. For most of these cheechakos coming through here now, two *months* would be a miracle."

"What'd you call them?"

"Cheechakos. Means greenhorns. Means you. If you survive your first winter, you'll be a sourdough."

Jason stepped outside, inspected the map. It was twenty-seven miles from the trading post, up and over the Chilkoot Pass and down to the first big lake on the other side, Lake Lindeman. Four miles long, Lindeman was connected to a much longer lake—Lake Bennett— by a mile of river. At the head of both lakes, an *X* was marked, with the inscription BUILD BOATS. His brothers would be building theirs at the head of Lake Bennett, where the trail over White Pass came in. People coming over the Chilkoot would build boats at the head of Lake Lindeman, then float to Bennett and beyond.

He'd lost twelve days, he realized. Twelve days ago he'd waved good-bye to Jack London only a few hundred yards from this very spot where he now stood.

He'd chosen wrong. If he'd gone over the Chilkoot, he would have arrived at Lake Bennett about the time his brothers got there over White Pass. But how could he have known?

Still, he should be okay. It was August 13, and his brothers had gotten to Lake Bennett on the fifth. He had a twenty-seven mile hike to Lake Lindeman, another six miles to reach his brothers. Without doubt he could reach them before they'd been at their boatbuilding for two weeks. He could still make it before they left. He had to.

## ELEVEN

Jason whistled to King and quickened his step as they started out along the wagon road from Dyea. It was crowded with Klondikers carrying loads on their backs and pulling hand sleds. To his surprise, he saw more than a few strings of packhorses, as well as horses pulling freight wagons and sledges. Hadn't he heard that horses couldn't go over the Chilkoot?

There was room to skirt the slow spots and nobody minded that he was trying to go fast. This trail didn't have the stench of defeat and death all over it. Everyone was talking about how hard the pass was going to be, especially the last, straight-up pitch called the Golden Stairs, but nobody was saying it couldn't be done.

The wagon road wound through meadows blazing with waist-high fireweed, crossed and recrossed the gravelly river among groves of cottonwood, birch, and spruce. Five miles up the valley the road crossed the river at the limit of navigation. The far shore was thick with Indian canoes. The packers—Tlingit men, women, boys, girls—were loading the packs they were going to carry over the pass.

Within a mile Jason passed through an encampment called Canyon City, and beyond that he entered the narrow canyon of the Dyea River, no more than fifty feet wide and cluttered with boulders and driftpiles. It was gloomy in the gorge with a drizzle setting in and the daylight going down, but after two miles the canyon was behind him and he landed in a busy place called Pleasant Camp. It had obviously been named by someone with a sense of humor—it was swampy and infested with mosquitoes. He pitched his tarp, cut spruce boughs for bedding, and brought out his dry supper as well as a dried salmon for King. The husky curled up next to him, happy to be scratched and petted.

At first light Jason was moving again, anxious to catch a glimpse of the infamous Chilkoot Pass. By midmorning he'd reached another tent and hut metropolis, Sheep Camp, at the end of the wagon road. Here the thick coastal forest gave way to knee-high spruces, tundra, and rock. Here the endless line of Klondikers and hired packers ascended the steep push up Long Hill—four miles long—that would lead them to the bottom of the Chilkoot and the final climb.

Up, up, Jason climbed in pursuit of the snow line. Klondikers stepping out of the trail to rest spared the breath to admire King. "Now, that's a dog." "How much is he carrying?" "Is your husky for sale?"

The last question was the most frequent. "Nope," Jason would say, "he's my partner."

At last Jason crowned the top of Long Hill. Here was

yet another tent city in a bowl at the foot of the encircling peaks. Directly across the bowl was the sight of a life-time—a stream of stampeders marching straight up for the sky, through rockslides and snowfields, at an angle that seemed impossible. The procession was aimed for a towering notch between two peaks, so high above that it seemed he'd fall backward looking at it. "The Golden Stairs," he heard someone say. "The stairs to the gold."

"Chilkoot Pass," Jason said under his breath. It was worse than he had pictured.

This last encampment before the summit, all congested with stampeders and mounded outfits, was called the Scales. Here the packers weighed everything and raised their rates for the foot traffic over the pass. The packhorses, mules, and burros were turned around. From this point on, everyone walked.

Jason found a spot to unpack the husky and himself, then lay back in the wildflowers and the sunshine for a few minutes. He drank from the creek, ate some jerky and dried apples. His shoulders felt like pincushions.

"Ready, King? This is it."

At the foot of the slope Jason joined the human lock-step up the Chilkoot—Klondikers lined up heel-to-toe. Within a minute his lungs were burning and he was gasping for air. He was afraid for the man in front of him, bent double under the weight of a gargantuan load that was heavy enough without the seven-foot sled that was lashed to the outside. The man's every breath sounded like a death wheeze.

Before long the trail left the rocks and started up the arrow-straight gully through the dirty snow remaining from the previous winter. The August day was hot despite the snow underfoot.

With so many coming behind, no one dared to stop moving. The lockstep proceeded at a snail's pace up, up, and up. To Jason's right, stampeders returning from the pass for another load were sledding down vertical chutes on their rumps.

Finally, a place to step out of line, breathe all the air he wanted, slow his heart, admire the view of the Scales far below and the peaks all around. King's tongue was lolling, but his eyes were burning bright.

Back in line. "We're halfway up," he encouraged the husky while he still had the breath. "Halfway up the Golden Stairs."

With every staggering step he took, his brothers came more clearly into focus. It had been over eleven months now since he'd seen them.

How much farther can the top possibly be?

Took off with my $500, did you? Nice boat you've fashioned here. Oh, I forgive you. Let's go find that gold in the creekbeds, thick as cheese in a sandwich.

And here, finally, was the summit! ENTERING CANADA, a small sign proclaimed.

Jason's heart was hammering, his lungs screaming for air. He reached to stroke the dog's head. "We made it," he gasped.

The summit was cluttered with mounds of gear, packing crates, and sleds. He stepped aside, and King with him, and watched the human highway go by: a Tlingit girl no older than he, bent under a heavy load; a man with one arm pulling a hand sled; a woman who looked seventy, speaking German. She was wearing a long dress, miraculously clean, with a lace apron.

Below on the Yukon side lay a mountain lake surrounded by rocks fallen from the peaks. Crater Lake, his map said. Still a ways to go before Lake Lindeman. "All downhill from here to Dawson City," Jason told the husky.

The weather was turning, and fast. A wall of sleet was sweeping through the pass and down onto the lake. Jason pulled out the oilskin suit he'd found in Skagway and put it on, then battened down the canvas flaps over the husky's panniers.

A minute later the sleet caught him, but he was ready.

He put Crater Lake behind him, then Long Lake. Finally he could see trees again, down below. Dusk was gathering as the tip of Lake Lindeman came into view. The tents around the inlet far below were thick, like a flock of seagulls.

Along the creek rushing toward Lindeman, Klondikers were carrying logs on their shoulders despite the late hour.

Jason walked through the tent city and approached the lakeshore. Men were still in the saw pits whipsawing lumber in the rain. Along the shore, skeletons of boats, dozens of them, were taking shape. Jason planned to walk the distance around Lake Lindeman to Lake Bennett, where he expected to find his brothers building their boat.

He kept going until the dark stopped him a mile around the east shore of the lake. There, under spruce cover, he pitched his tarp and slept soundly, knowing that only five miles remained.

At first light he was racing along Lindeman's shore with King on his heels. The lake was pointed north like an arrow and so was he. Nothing could stop him now. Finally Lindeman was pinching shut, and here was the

One Mile River flowing out of it down to Lake Bennett, down to where his brothers would be.

As he approached Lake Bennett, a bright turquoise jewel, his heart was racing. It had been nearly a month since that day in New York City when he'd held up a newspaper and shouted out the discovery.

Across the continent, then north a thousand miles and more. He couldn't wait to see the look on his brothers' faces.

Jason came over a rise, and now he could see Lake Bennett's tent city and the boatworks below. Just then he caught sight of another trail, a quarter mile or so on his right, that also led into Bennett. A man over there was putting a pistol to a horse's head. The pistol shot cracked and the horse collapsed grotesquely. The meadow on both sides of the trail was strewn with the bodies of horses.

This was the end of the Dead Horse Trail, he realized. Here was the prize for the horses who had survived it. He was sickened all over again. He cursed under his breath and kept going.

Along the lake Jason found twenty or so boats under construction. He ran from one to the next, each time certain his brothers' faces would come into focus. Time after time he encountered the faces of strangers.

"Do you know the Hawthorn brothers, Abe and Ethan?" he began to ask.

No one did. He started describing them.

Finally he got a nod from a man with a droopy mustache. "From Seattle? Sawmill experience? In their twenties?"

"That's them. I'm their brother."

"Luckiest sons of guns I've met in my life."

"What? Where are they?"

"Never even had to build a boat, those two. They hit it off with two fellows who'd started building a boat here before news of the Klondike strike ever got to the States. The boat was all but finished, but the two who built it were short on grub. Your brothers showed up with two thousand pounds of food. Traded five hundred pounds of it for a boat ride to Dawson City."

"You mean they're gone?"

"They ain't only gone, kid, they're halfway there by now. Did they know you was coming?"

"They didn't have any idea."

"That's a real shame. Those brothers of yours are at the head of this entire stampede, if that's any consolation."

It wasn't. His disappointment was so deep, it didn't help at all. Surprising them, stepping into the boat with them, had been everything for so long.

Now he had nothing. He was stranded.

"Busted, by God," he said between his teeth.

He was utterly confused. He looked around, noticed the husky sniffing the wind. He saw that the birches along the shore were turning red. It was an ominous harbinger of winter.

The man who'd met his brothers buttoned up his sheepskin coat and turned back to his work. "Can I help you?" Jason offered. "In exchange for space on your boat?"

The man shook his head. "If you don't have an outfit, I think you'd better head home, son. I'm sorry."

"I have nowhere to go. My brothers are my only family."

"I'm sorry," the man repeated, and turned his back on him.

Jason tried everywhere he saw a boat under construction. He offered to work in the saw pits in exchange for transportation to Dawson City. He told them he'd carpentered in St. Louis, which was true.

He was offered only a cup of coffee. In a daze, he retraced his steps back alongside the roily One Mile River. He would ask the parties building boats at Lake Lindeman. Maybe someone there would take him on.

At the head of the One Mile River, he sat on a rocky bluff with King beside him and watched the glassy current pouring out of Lake Lindeman into the white water below.

After an hour, he still hadn't moved. He was exhausted, but even more, he was drained of the spirit that made him who he was. He didn't know, he might even be beaten.

Then he heard shouts. They were coming from a number of people running toward him along the lakeshore. One of them stopped for a second to point toward something out in the lake.

There was a canoe out there, coming on fast. Jason thought immediately of Jamie and her father. Could it be them, traveling fast and light?

"They're going to run it!" Jason heard from the Klondikers scrambling to join him on the bluff.

Jason was soon surrounded by two dozen people yelling and pointing. "Look at all those rocks!" "They'll never make it!"

Now he could see the enormous gray beard distinctly, the girl slender as a willow, Jamie's black hair.

Another few minutes and here they came, paddles flashing, right down the tongue of the current sweeping into the river—the girl from Swift Water at the bow, her face all fierce determination, the bush poet at the stern, steering gracefully, with the joyful grin of a man in his own element. To the surprise of all, amid cheers and the waving of hats and the barking of a big male husky, they passed below without leaving so much as a smudge of green paint on the rocks.

Jason sat staring at the rapids in the One Mile River long after the Klondikers had gone back to their camps. He couldn't believe that Jamie and Homer had come and gone so suddenly, so quickly, without even knowing he was here. It was so hard to accept, that he wasn't going to be able to follow the water to Dawson City. "It's only a three-week paddle," he could hear Jamie saying.

At the boatworks at Lake Lindeman, there were now more than thirty boats under construction. He explained himself, tried again and again. The answer was always the same: He had nothing to offer.

His brothers would have fed him. Why should anyone else?

Jason realized he was standing out in the pouring rain and hadn't even reached for his oilskin suit. King rolled the whites of his eyes toward him, then looked away.

Seattle? he wondered. See if Mrs. Beal had a room for him? Maybe go back to that sheep camp in Wyoming where he'd worked last fall?

He saw nothing to do but start back. He could probably find a job on one of the steamers, stoking coal. "Klondike or bust," he muttered bitterly.

Five hundred miles short of the Klondike, he'd gone bust.

He still couldn't believe it.

## TWELVE

Back on the Alaska side of the pass, at the Scales, Jason took one last look at the human cavalcade inching up the Chilkoot to the sky. Close by, chuckling erupted from a cluster of Indian packers. Three Tlingits were enjoying the spectacle of a young white man about to shoulder an immense pack and start up the Golden Stairs, clad only in his bright red long underwear.

The day was unusually warm, making the costume a sensible one for climbing the Chilkoot, but it *was* a striking sight.

Suddenly Jason recognized that tangle of hair with one lock falling across the forehead, and those broad square shoulders. "Jack London!" he cried.

"Jason!"

Here was the familiar infectious grin, the laughter in

the Californian's gray-blue eyes. Here was an old friend, though Jason had known him only briefly.

Jack stepped off the trail. "Sit down and tell me how you came by that beautiful animal. I'll take a few more minutes before my last run up the Stairs. *Run*, hah!"

Jason began where Jack had asked, and told about the man who'd lost his reason, drowning his dogs on the White Pass Trail. London's deep-set eyes burned at the telling. He winced at the gruesome end the man had made of his life and shook his head grimly, looking at the ground as Jason described the carnage of dead horses and the new name for the trail.

"What about your brothers, then, if you were turned back? Are you on your way over the Chilkoot to find them?"

Jason had to tell him that he'd already been over the Chilkoot to Lake Bennett, and failed.

"If I'd only known!" London exclaimed. "Two days ago, we took on a new partner who had only what he was carrying on his back, same as you."

"You did? What happened?"

"My brother-in-law, Captain Shepard... You remember him. His heart and his rheumatism wouldn't allow him to continue, no matter how game he was for the adventure. He's turned back, gone home to San Francisco. We took in an old salt named Tarwater...."

"He's taken over Captain Shepard's outfit?"

"Only clothing and such; the rest we left back in Canyon City. Tarwater intends one way or another simply to squeak through. . . . I talked my three partners into taking him to Dawson City purely for the stories he tells. Among us, we've got around thirty-five hundred pounds of grub. The Mounties down at Tagish Lake, we're told, want to see seven hundred pounds per man, so we've got him covered for customs. Once he gets to Dawson, Tarwater will be on his own."

"Any chance I could sneak on board, and King here, too?"

Jack shook his head decisively. "Five men and four outfits will about sink us. My partners would execute me if I added someone else; it really would be dangerous."

"Do you have your boat built on the other side?"

"By no means, but as soon as Sloper or Goodman or I finish lugging our outfits to Lindeman, we can help Thompson take down trees, build a saw pit, and start making some lumber. I've knocked about in small boats enough to name their parts in my sleep, and Merritt Sloper's actually built them."

"How far have you moved the rest of your outfit?"

"It's on top of the pass, barely onto the Canadian side. Do you realize that very few of these thousands of people are going to beat winter to Dawson City?"

"Not get through?"

"Not this year. They're going to be camping at Lindeman or Bennett all winter, or else they'll retreat to Dyea or Skagway. There's just not time. It's going to take most people two and three months to lug their outfits to Lindeman."

"Do they know?"

"Oh, they know. If they're carrying their outfits on their own backs—and almost everyone is—believe me, they've figured out the cruel mathematics of it."

"Can you beat freeze-up yourself?"

"I think I have a sporting chance. At the beginning, I put my pencil to paper and figured out what I had to do to complete my portage by the end of August. Four times a day, I carry one hundred and fifty pounds three miles forward."

"You can do that?"

"I've become a human pack animal, Jason. I've been walking twenty-four miles a day, twelve of it loaded down like a mule."

"You can't weigh much more than a hundred and fifty yourself."

"Hundred and sixty-five when I left home."

"When's the latest you can have your boat finished and still start in time?"

"By the fifteenth of September, we hear, we need to be on the water and rowing hard for the Golden City."

"You'll make it, I know you will."

"What about you, though? I can see it in your eyes, Jason. You're like me. More than anything, you want to know what's around the bend and over the next hill, don't you?"

"You know I do."

"You and I, we're the kind who relish the hardest work if there's purpose to it and we're not being exploited by the lazy rich. Why, I'd stand up to God and man and the devil to be able to choose my own road, and I know you would too."

"You know I would! I'm never going back to a place like that cannery, if that's what you mean. Never."

London's eyes were lit with a peculiar fire. "Listen, then: You can still have your chance at the Klondike. I've been dreading having to return to Canyon City and dispose of Captain Shepard's outfit. It's right there, neatly covered with a tarp, with his brand all over it. If you had an outfit, if you were willing to lug it over the pass . . . with a dog that could carry heavy, like yours, to help you out . . ."

"Yes?"

"I'm thinking. . . . If you had a complete outfit on the shore of Lindeman, and were willing to make yourself useful in the saw pits—that's inhumanly brutal work—you'd stand a chance that a boatbuilding crew would take you on. They'd add the benefit of your labor without drawing down their grub. It might be worth a try. Even if you don't hook up with a boat this fall, you'd have the outfit for another try come breakup."

Jason thought about it. He didn't have to think long. "I'd do it—of course I'd do it. But I'm flat busted. I could make some money carpentering in Skagway or Dyea, but by the time I had enough to buy Shepard's outfit, you'd—"

"No, no—I didn't make myself clear. The outfit is yours if you want it."

"You couldn't do that, Jack."

"Sure I could. It's not even worth my time to try to sell it piecemeal. It would give me pleasure to give it to you, Jason."

Jack London opened a pouch on the outside of his packsack, pulled out an envelope. "The inventory is all listed inside. You'll see I've scratched out the stove, shovels, the sled, the tent, and the boatbuilding tools—I've taken those. The outfit should weigh no more than eleven or twelve hundred pounds."

London pulled out a pencil, scribbled a message, signed with a flourish, and dated it. "There, it's done. Everything with the Shepard brand belongs to Jason Hawthorn. You'll have no trouble locating the outfit—CS with lightning bolts on both sides—under a big spruce down at Canyon City."

"This is twice you've helped me."

"Say, you don't have any mind fodder, do you? It's

going to be a long winter, and I've got only six volumes in my library—Darwin, Huxley, Spencer, Dante, Milton, and Marx."

Jason brightened. "I do have something. I have a Kipling—*The Seven Seas*."

"You don't mean it! The man's prose is superb. That book would be worth its weight in gold—a fair trade for Captain Shepard's outfit, I'd say."

They shook on their trade and their friendship.

With his Kipling stowed, Jack hoisted his pack to a knee-high rock, squatted under it, reached for his walking stick, then stood up, muscles rippling. "My twelfth and last run up the Chilkoot," he declared through gritted teeth. "Come see me when you get to Lindeman, Jason, and wave me off to the goldfields!"

Jason watched the striking figure in scarlet underwear join the line at the bottom of the Chilkoot. He followed Jack London's slow progress up the staggeringly steep slope as he alternately scanned the description of Captain Shepard's outfit. Jason Hawthorn's outfit now.

Under FOODSTUFFS: "400 lbs. flour, 50 lbs. cornmeal, 50 lbs. oatmeal, 35 lbs. rice, 100 lbs. beans, 100 lbs. sugar, 8 lbs. baking powder, 200 lbs. bacon, 2 lbs. soda, 36 yeast cakes, 15 lbs. salt, 1 lb. pepper, 25 lbs. tinned fish, 25 lbs. coffee, 5 lbs. tea, 4 dozen tins condensed milk, 25 cans lard, 25 lbs. apples, 25 lbs. peaches, 25 lbs. apricots, 10 lbs. plums, 50 lbs. onions, 50 lbs. potatoes, 15 lbs. soup vegetables. All fruits and vegetables dried."

Under HARD GOODS: "40 lbs. candles, 5 bars laundry soap, 60 boxes matches, match dry-safe, gold pan, 3 nesting buckets, cup, cutlery, 2 fry pans, coffeepot, light and heavy sacks, sewing and first-aid kits, whetstone, hatchet, file, ax, rifle, ammunition, butcher knife, 200 feet rope."

Jason looked up. The bright red patch that was Jack was halfway up, still inching higher.

He looked back down at the list. The full measure of the man's generosity began to sink in. Here was the means to join a Klondike partnership.

Over the shoulder of the Chilkoot went a tiny patch of red. A minute later Jason was starting down Long Hill. "We aren't retreating," he assured the husky. "We aren't beaten by a long shot."

## THIRTEEN

Under a big spruce at Canyon City, Jason found the out-fit as promised. At first light on the eighteenth of August, he headed north once again. He was carrying seventy-five pounds and the husky fifty; he'd weighed it all out at the blacksmith's at Canyon City.

Half a mile up the wagon road, his pack already felt like lead, but his walking staff helped, and he found he could perch the pack on a waist-high boulder when he had to get the weight off his shoulders. King, with his long tongue lolling like a wolf's, was thriving on the work.

Jason employed London's strategy: Carry three miles up the trail, cache everything under the tarp. Return three miles downhill with an empty pack. Load up, turn around, climb.

He made four trips that first day. Together, he and

King advanced five hundred pounds three miles up the trail. They'd walked twenty-four miles, twelve of it under loads.

He was exhausted, but he'd done it. Don't lie down, he warned himself. Take the ax, find firewood, start a fire, cook up some grub, make some tea. Cut boughs to sleep on while there's still light. Sleep.

Every day, do it again.

And he did. Whenever he started feeling like a pack-horse, he'd think about Jack's hundred and fifty pounds.

Just keep moving. You have become an ant. You are one ant in this endless train of ants. You are tireless. You can lift twenty times your weight. You don't need to see beyond your antennas. Back and forth, back and forth, back and forth. Stay in line and keep moving!

One day he found himself marching behind a wizened old man with a grindstone strapped to a pack-board, a large grindstone. Jason couldn't help but ask what it was for.

"Lots of miners gonna need picks and shovels and axes sharpened," the weary old man explained, panting. "Pay me in nuggets, they will—I done it in the Cariboo and the Cassiar."

The following day, as Jason leaned against a boulder at trailside and struggled for breath, he saw King's erect ears swivel around. The husky froze, alertly studying something on the slope below.

"What do you see, King?"

Here came the strangest sight, a team of five long-haired goats pulling a sledge with a camera and tripod lashed to a big boxy contraption.

A few minutes later Jason met the young man who was wrangling the goats, as he in turn stopped to wheeze for breath. His name was Eric Hegg, and he was a pho-

tographer from Bellingham, Washington. The boxy contraption turned out to be his darkroom. Hegg wasn't
even interested in the gold. His gold was going to be the
photos he was taking. He was headed over the Chilkoot
and down to Dawson City just to photograph the rush.

One of the times Jason was overnighting at Sheep
Camp he pitched his tarp next to a Canadian party from
Lake Winnipeg. They waved him over so they could
admire King, then invited him for bannock—simple
camp bread, more like sweet cake with the berries
they'd thrown in. Before he left they told him how to
make it. The batter was a combination of flour, lard, and
baking powder, all of which he had in strong supply.

The Canadians even showed him what berries he
was after: high- and low-bush cranberries, raspberries,
blueberries. And he learned a valuable tip for starting
fires in wet weather: Keep a supply of birch bark handy.

In the morning Jason began the push up Long Hill
to the Scales. From now until the top of the Chilkoot he
faced steep climbing all the way.

Through every sort of weather, he and the husky
kept it up: nine backbreaking trips up Long Hill, nine
agonizing times up the Golden Stairs. The last time up
the pass, on the first day of September, he was wearing
his winter clothes and winter boots. They climbed the
Stairs in a blinding snowstorm with flakes the size of silver dollars. When they reached the top, fifteen inches of
new snow covered the tarp over the outfit they'd
brought in stages to the summit. The sight of the mountains under snow scared him. "All downhill now," he told
King bravely. "All we have to do is move twelve hundred
pounds nine miles and catch a ride."

The snow melted, but hard freezes came every night.

The tundra grasses around Crater Lake and Long Lake flamed orange and red, and by the time he'd moved the outfit far enough along to see Lake Lindeman below, the birches along its shores were all blazing scarlet.

All along the trail, outfits were piled high as houses. When would breakup come? people were asking, figuring they'd have to spend the winter.

The end of May seemed to be the answer.

Jason already knew he wasn't going to ride out the winter at Lindeman. Even if he had a proper tent and a Klondike stove, even if he was willing to go back to Dyea or Skagway and find work until he could buy them, even if he were to carry them back over the Chilkoot, he couldn't possibly sit still for eight months. For him that would be eight years.

Maybe another man in Jack's party had taken sick, dropped out.

It was the eighth of September when he reached the tent city at Lake Lindeman with the first portion of his outfit. Pistol shots and running Klondikers drew him to the lakeshore, where hundreds were seeing off a newly launched skiff.

"How many have been launching?" he asked the first person he saw, a woman at a makeshift laundry.

"For the last week, five to ten a day."

Running to a high point, he counted the boats under construction. Close to sixty!

He found Jack on the bottom end of a whipsaw, making lumber in the saw pits. The man standing up above was Big Jim Goodman. On every upstroke, the fresh sawdust fell into Jack's face, though he'd pulled his hobo cap low over his forehead.

Jack recognized him, came out of the pits for a

moment, and gestured toward the mountainsides all covered with snow. "Close contest!" he exclaimed. "Winter's coming hard."

"I brought my first load. The rest is close—Long Lake. Anybody looking for a partner?"

"No change with us . . . but ask around. . . . Good luck!"

Jason did ask. He asked at every single boat. He even started offering half a share in the claim he would stake in the Klondike.

No room.

Back for another load. Don't give up yet.

In three more days his outfit was complete and within a stone's throw of the lakeshore. It was all here. All he needed now was a miracle.

Jack's skiff, the twenty-seven-foot *Yukon Belle*, was fully framed and now the lumber was going on—soft green spruce boards an inch thick. It was a flat-bottomed boat, pointed at the bow and squared off at the stern, six feet or so across the beam.

Whenever a boat was finished, word was hollered and Jason joined dozens of Klondikers who ran from all directions to lift it into the water where it could be loaded.

At almost all the boatworks, he heard worried talk about the One Mile River, the narrow stretch of water connecting Lindeman and Bennett. Almost all the parties who had launched up through the first week of September had rowed down to the end of Lake Lindeman, then portaged around the One Mile River. It meant completely unloading the boats, packing the outfits around on foot, skidding the skiffs a mile on logs over extremely uneven terrain.

But now freeze-up was like an avenger on their

heels. The day before, six boats had reached the far end of Lindeman. Three had tried to run the One Mile River to avoid the time-consuming portage. Two of them had broken to splinters on the rocks. No one was drowned, but eleven men had lost everything and gone bust before they even reached Lake Bennett.

Now there were thirty boats left on the shore, with very few days remaining before the middle of September. A Yellow Legs hiked up from Lake Bennett to spread the word that any launch after the next few days would have little chance of making Dawson City. Lake Laberge, a thirty-mile-long deadwater stretch of the Yukon River, was especially prone to early freeze-up. Outfits were going to be inspected extra carefully at customs, just below Tagish Lake, at Fort Sifton. "Seven hundred pounds of foodstuffs per person, or you *will* be turned back."

Five boats launched on the fourteenth, two on the fifteenth. Crude improvised sails appeared; the slightest advantage might spell the margin of victory over the ice. On the night of the fifteenth it snowed on the tent city at Lake Lindeman. Now the mountainsides rising from the lake and into the distance were entirely shrouded with snow.

On the sixteenth, Jason helped to launch and load the *Yukon Belle*. He was going to run around the side of the lake to see Jack and the others attempt the One Mile River. They'd decided they had to run it—no time to portage—and Jack was going to be doing the steering with the big sweep oar at the stern.

The time had come to say good-bye again. As Jack took his hand, the Californian looked as chagrined as he looked exhausted. "I was sure hoping you'd find a spot on one of the boats."

Jason fought to keep his head up. "It was worth a try."

"What do you think you'll do now?"

"I don't know," Jason allowed. "I just don't know."

They wished each other luck. Without really believing it, Jason added, "I'll see you in the Golden City!" then started around the shore of the lake.

He and King were halfway around the shore when the pistol shots rang out signaling the launch of the *Yukon Belle*. "We're in for a show," he said to the husky.

Jason took his position on the rocky bluff above the lake's outlet, the same vantage point from which he'd seen Jamie and her father make their unforgettable run. Here came the *Yukon Belle*, with Big Jim Goodman pushing at the oars and Jack standing at the stern with the long sweep oar in hand. The other three—tall, thin, orange-whiskered Fred Thompson; the small, wiry Merritt Sloper; and their graybeard, Tarwater—were hunkered low and hanging on tight.

Down the glassy tongue of water pouring out of the lake they came. From the corner of his eye, Jason suddenly became aware of a stranger pounding headlong down the shore. A young man of twenty-five or so, the fellow was wearing a plaid mackinaw like Jason's, but much cleaner, and a new-looking felt hat. "Got to see the route they pick!" the stranger exclaimed, all out of breath, as he reached Jason's shoulder.

The skiff passed almost beneath them and shot downstream into the white water.

It was close, so close. Several times the *Belle* seemed certain to crash on the rocks midriver. Braced at the stern and leaning into the sweep oar with all of his might, Jack steered them around each of the deadly obstacles.

Jason cheered them on their way, and they were gone.

"And now it's my turn," the stranger said nervously. "I've left my canoe up the shore there. Came running to see this, and I'm glad I did."

"Canoe?" Jason repeated, barely listening.

"I had it packed over the pass. I just got here—came all the way from Boston. Still seems strange to me that the rivers up here run north. Everything's different up here."

Now Jason was fully alert. "Take me and my dog with you! I've got a world of grub if you need any, and I'll help out all along the way."

The man waved him off. "I'm overloaded as it is. But would you like to make a little money?"

"I guess," Jason allowed through his disappointment.

"Wait for me at the bottom, then, with a rope."

"A rope? What for?"

"To fish me out if I spill," the man explained, greatly agitated. "Ten dollars. I'll pay ten dollars. Tell me quick—will you do it?"

"Of course I will, but . . ." Jason looked the stranger over. *Cheechako* was written all over him. "Are you sure you don't want to portage your outfit around the rapids?"

"No time!" the stranger cried, nearly frantic. "I'll do exactly as he did. You stay here. I'll be back with my canoe in twenty minutes."

The canoe was identical to Jamie and Homer Dunavant's—eighteen feet long and painted dark green. A beauty, but heavily loaded. Too heavy for these rapids, Jason thought.

The man jumped out of his canoe, pushed a ten-dollar bill and a coil of rope at Jason, then yelled, "I'll start in twenty minutes. Now go!"

Jason started briskly down the trail with King at his heels. They positioned themselves at the slow water below the rapids.

It wasn't long before Jason saw a flash of green upstream. It was the canoe, but the canoe had capsized. He caught sight of the man from Boston clawing to hang on. Odds and ends of the unfortunate's outfit came bobbing down the river, but most of it had sunk.

Jason threw the man the rope. "Busted, by God!" he sputtered when Jason hauled him out. "God help my wife and children!"

Still upside-down, the canoe was caught against the right bank not far downstream. So was the canoe paddle.

Suddenly Jason could see his chance. Finally, his lucky break. "I'll give you your money back if you let me have the canoe."

The man cried, "Give it, then! The canoe is yours."

All the next day and the following morning Jason carried his own outfit along the shore past the rapids, then packed it into the canoe. He loaded up as much of his supplies as he could until he started losing too much freeboard between the water and the gunwales. It was easy enough to picture the wind-driven waves out on the lake swamping the canoe.

He had all his clothes on board, the cookware, the hatchet, the ax, the whetstone, two buckets, the rifle, the ammunition, candles, matches, his blankets, his tarp, the rope, King's remaining salmon, and as much food for himself as he could fit in.

As for the rest, he had to leave it behind.

Jason packed carefully, tied everything in, slid the

rifle under the ropes, then showed the husky his spot at the bow. King jumped into the canoe and Jason took his own place at the stern.

He could hardly believe he was finally under way, paddling onto Lake Bennett under the snow-shrouded mountains. It was the eighteenth of September. The cloud line was halfway down to the lake, gloomy like a permanent fixture.

King stood with his front feet on the little shelf under the bow, looking north and sniffing the wind.

"I'm counting on you, partner," Jason told him.

The wind was out of the north, blowing against them. How was he going to get past the Yellow Legs?

This was crazy, he realized, but he'd come too far not to try it.

Everyone this far north was more than half-crazy, including him.

PART TWO

# Down the Yukon

N

ALASKA

Fortymile

DAWSON
CITY

Klondike R.

Bonanza Ck.

Eldorado
Ck.

Stewart R.

UNITED STATES
CANADA

White R.

YUKON RIVER

Pelly R.

Five Fingers
Rapids

Nordenskjold R.

Little Salmon R.

Big
Salmon R.

UPPER YUKON RIVER-
LAKE BENNETT
TO DAWSON CITY

0                    100
Scale in Miles.

Lake Laberge

Miles Canyon

White Horse
Rapids

Marsh Lake

Fort Sifton

Lake Bennett

Tagish Lake

## FOURTEEN

For three days Jason battled blustery Lake Bennett, a glacial spear aimed at the North Star. When it seemed he'd never have its rough and icy water behind him, the turquoise lake left its mountain corridor with a sudden bend to the east. Jason found himself in a narrows, with the wind for once at his back. He paddled hard to take advantage.

Ahead, rifle shots. Around a bend, the channel was choked with caribou, many hundreds of them, swimming across the neck of water that connected Bennett to the next lake, Tagish. Small explosions of smoke and the flash of paddles along the waterline drew his attention to the source of the shots: Indian birch-bark canoes in motion alongside the mass of surging heads and the forest of antlers.

Jason paddled closer and watched as a man tied a rope around the antlers of a dead caribou. The Indian motioned quickly toward Jason's rifle atop his outfit, then nodded toward the herd as if to say, Help yourself.

At the thought of fresh meat for himself and the husky, Jason readied the rifle. Point-blank, he aimed at a fine-looking caribou as the animal rolled its eyes fearfully toward him.

Jason wasn't ready for the overwhelming blast in his ears or the recoil against his shoulder. At least he hadn't wounded the animal; it had died instantly. He tied the free end of the canoe's stern line to the antlers and paddled for the north shore, where caribou by the dozens were being dressed out on the beach.

A white man with broad yellow suspenders who was watching the spectacle stepped forward to help him beach his canoe and haul the caribou onto land. His name was Higgins, and he was from the trading post at Caribou Crossing, a village close by. "Anyone behind you?" Higgins wondered.

"I saw half a dozen sails yesterday and two this morning."

"Some will move forward as they finish their boats, I'm thinking, and make their winter camps along the shores of Tagish and Marsh Lakes. I expect you're still going to try to beat the ice to Dawson City?"

Jason nodded. "And I don't know the first thing about how to deal with this carcass. Could you lend me a hand?"

Drawing a sheath knife, Higgins made quick work of freeing the hindquarters. "I suggest you take just these—you don't appear to have room for more meat and won't have time to dry it anyway."

Jason brought his map of the Yukon's upper reaches from his back pocket and asked, "When do you figure I'll reach customs?"

"Depends on the wind. Fort Sifton's right there along the Tagish River, which is the few miles of current between Tagish Lake and Marsh Lake."

"Which side is the fort on?"

"Your left—the west. Worried about the Mounties' seven-hundred-pound grub requirement, eh?"

"I am. I might have only five hundred."

"Through August they were lax. They'd huff and puff, but they let men through with next to nothing. One fellow had a flute and a knapsack. Now they're talking about raising the minimum to a thousand pounds."

Jason paddled on. It was strange, after having been trapped for so long among the hordes of stampeders, to suddenly whisk past them and find himself alone in this vast country. His brothers seemed so far away, yet he knew he was at last closing the gap.

With the wind at his back, Jason sped into and along the windy west arm of Tagish Lake. He squinted into the distance to see if he might sight a canoe paddling his way.

What if it was a Mountie? What would he do?

He didn't know. Would they really turn him back over a few hundred pounds?

Jason camped where this west arm of the lake was joined by a much longer one running up from the south. He feasted along with the husky on skillet-fried caribou steaks and bannock sprinkled with cranberries. In the morning, caribou steaks and bannock again, then a day's paddle north against the wind to the foot of Tagish Lake by dusk.

He was within a few miles of Fort Sifton.

They might very well turn him back, especially because he was young and traveling alone.

He couldn't take the chance.

Bundled against the cold, Jason started paddling several hours after the sun had set. The hours of daylight had already shrunk dramatically. The whole of the sky was ablaze with stars, and their reflection off the water provided sufficient light. He'd never seen so many stars in his life. The climate was much drier here on the Canadian side. It wasn't raining all the time; the trees weren't massive; the air was clear as crystal.

Jason paddled in the frosty stillness down the slow-moving Tagish River, hugging the east bank. When he spied the dim outlines of the flagpole and the log cabins on the opposite shore, he let the canoe drift.

King knew they were being stealthy and remained frozen at the bow, studying the buildings intently. The cabins were slipping by; Jason was holding his breath. There was no motion there and no sound anywhere but the ghostly hooting of an owl in the distance.

With the fort behind them, a ghostly dancing curtain of yellows and greens appeared from horizon to horizon, shimmering and changing shape from moment to moment. Jason had heard about the aurora but never seen it. The husky was watching it too, and the hair stood up along King's spine.

"The northern lights, King."

Jason's breath in the cold made an eerie vapor that sank toward the surface of the river and trailed away.

He'd been in unusual spots tramping across the country, but nothing like this. Nothing like paddling alone into the far interior of the North.

It must be at least midnight. He could still see, so why stop?

Once onto Marsh Lake, he made out three different camps of Klondikers by their white canvas tents. In the silence he floated past them.

He was no longer the caboose on the last train trying to reach Dawson.

For hours, the aurora provided even more light, and it mesmerized him with a fierce joy that redoubled his determination.

At a spur of land jutting into the lake, he made camp finally, and slept. With the first light King was stirring. Jason roused himself from his blankets. The tarp was frozen stiff, and frost coated the blueberry bushes.

That day Jason passed four more parties on Marsh Lake. His canoe was much faster than the skiffs, unless they had a following wind and were able to improvise a sail, but it was almost all headwinds now.

Paddling to his utmost, he put Marsh Lake behind him in a day and camped where a river poured out of the lake. Checking his map, he verified that the pale green river that began on this spot was none other than the mighty Yukon.

It was the twenty-third of September as he started north on the great river. The sky above was filled with vees of noisy geese and swans and cranes fleeing the country where he was headed. The aspens and birches on the hillsides were at their peak of yellow and red, while the brush on the top glowed a deep crimson purple. Along the river itself, the dense cottonwoods and willows flamed bright gold.

The middle of the day was so warm he had to peel off his wool shirt and paddle in his flannel undershirt. He

grinned, remembering Jack in his red underwear climbing the Chilkoot.

Two, three weeks at most, he'd rendezvous with his
brothers in the Golden City, then stake his claim. Within
a month, he'd be shoveling gold.

## FIFTEEN

The next morning, Indian summer was only a memory. A gale from the north had blown all night and sent the golds and reds to the ground. Entire stands of aspen and birch stood gray against an ashen sky.

As Jason paddled on, he listened carefully for the sound of fast water. DANGEROUS RAPIDS, the map said. The last thing he wanted to do was paddle into the white water of Miles Canyon by accident.

As he rounded a high prominent bluff, he spied a piece of red calico tied on a willow along the bank. A warning?

Yes. The box canyon loomed downriver, its dark walls of basalt a hundred feet high. The narrowed river as it passed inside looked barely wider than fifty. Dozens of boats were tied to the shore in an eddy that pooled above the entrance to the canyon. Klondikers were portaging their outfits on their backs along a trail that led above the cliffs. Here began the most difficult five miles of the Yukon, the part Jamie Dunavant had said a beginner couldn't manage in a canoe. Had Jamie and her father dared to run it?

With great difficulty, the Klondikers were skidding their heavy skiffs along the portage trail over logs placed across the path. "Let's go take a look," Jason suggested to the husky. "Find out what we're in for."

They walked along the very edge of the cliffs, looking down into the violent chute of foaming waves. After a quarter of a mile the gorge ended, but almost immediately a second one began. In between, as the river rushed out of the first gorge, it was consumed by surging boils and a monstrous whirlpool on a scale that reminded him of the boat-eating Charybdis of mythology.

On both sides of the whirlpool, eddies raced violently upstream against the cliffs. He could understand why everyone was portaging.

The second box canyon was a near duplicate of the first, only narrower. Together they totaled a mile. At the end of the mile, Jason could see boats down below putting back onto the river at the head of Squaw Rapids. He listened to the talk on the bluffs as Klondikers nervously discussed the water downstream. After Squaw Rapids, he learned, came even bigger waves in the White Horse Rapids, said to resemble a parade of white horses standing on their hind legs.

It was the narrow canyons that were the chief hazard—having your boat bashed against the walls, or spilling in the whirlpool in between the two canyons. Squaw and White Horse Rapids could be run, they said.

Not by canoe, Jason thought. Not by me.

Jason knew he'd have to portage the canyons, but if he took the time to portage Squaw and White Horse Rapids as well, he'd lose his race with winter for certain.

Jason's eyes were drawn back to the head of Squaw Rapids. He saw his answer. Several parties, unwilling to risk running the white water, were roping their boats down the edge of the rapids from the shore. That's what he would do, walk the canoe down on a short leash. But first he had to portage around the canyons.

Returning to his canoe at the head of Miles Canyon, Jason faced a thorny problem. There were a hundred men on this trail, yet he couldn't beg for help. Every one of them was in a desperate race against the ice. How was he to portage his canoe single-handed?

King was anxious to start down the trail. Would he pull? The madman on the Dead Horse Trail had said he wouldn't.

But if King would . . .

Jason brought out the husky's harness. King leaped in the air at the sight of it, nosed it, leaped again.

Won't pull, eh?

Jason attached the harness, then fifteen feet of rope running back from it to the canoe. With King out in front pulling, and him horsing the canoe as needs be over the skids . . .

It was worth a try.

Jason placed some logs across the path, pulled the canoe into position on top of them, found a few more logs to place across the trail ahead.

The Klondikers skidding the skiff ahead of them paused to study the arrangement, all grins.

"Pull, King!" Jason called.

In reply, the big husky simply wagged his tail.

The Klondikers laughed and went back to work.

Jason went to the husky, talked to him, took his harness in hand above his shoulder blades, and pulled. "Pull," Jason repeated. The canoe rolled forward a few inches. He repeated the demonstration again and again, then walked up the trail twenty feet ahead, turned around, and chanted, "Pull, King! Pull! Pull for me!"

And King pulled. Tentatively at first, but with encouragement, more and more, until the husky was pulling with all his might. Jason raced back to the rear of the canoe, picked up a log, and shuttled it to the front. "Pull!" Jason yelled, yanking with all his strength on the gunwales.

With the two of them working, the canoe moved along the trail much faster than he'd guessed it would. They were having an easier time of it, in fact, than the Klondikers in front of them, who were floundering with their big skiff.

At the break between canyons, Jason rested opposite the whirlpool. At the sound of men running on the trail behind him, he turned around and spied none other than Jack London pounding down the trail with the wiry Merritt Sloper close behind.

"Jason Hawthorn!" London cried. "You, *ahead* of me? What in the world? How did you manage it? And here I'd been picturing you stuck back at Lindeman. Now, here's a dog team worthy of legend, a one-dog team—the mighty King!"

Jason pulled the canoe out of the trail, and they swapped stories. Jack's party had been one of those he'd passed along Marsh Lake in the night.

London and Sloper studied the whirlpool, then trotted down the path to take a look at the second gorge. Jason and King had gone back to work and had advanced the canoe by fits and starts halfway along the trail above the second canyon when London and Sloper returned panting up the trail. They were joined by Thompson, Goodman, and Tarwater from upriver.

"Want to portage the canyon, Jack?" called orange-whiskered Fred Thompson. "Like everyone else?"

"Nothing doing, says my vote," Jack replied. "I've seen nothing we can't manage."

"Sure it can be done, eh, captain?" asked Big Jim Goodman.

London's eyes were blazing. "Two minutes saves us two days, maybe three."

"It might make the difference where we winter," put in Sloper.

The grizzled Tarwater had the last word. When Jack asked his opinion, he replied, "Been ponderin' so hard I ain't had time to think. But I'm game for the ride if you're the one drivin'."

They took their vote: unanimous in favor of the two-minute route. They were going to run Miles Canyon.

As his party started up the trail, Jack lingered for a moment. "Jason, it seems like we're always saying hello or good-bye."

"I'll see you in the Golden City; I'm sure of it."

"You've heard about Lake Laberge up ahead? The Yukon pools up there, for some inconvenient reason— the lake is thirty miles long, and they say it can ice over the last week in September."

"Any day now."

"Exactly. Don't lose any strokes with that paddle of yours until you get past Laberge. I'm counting on you to come up big."

"I will. Good luck to you in the canyon!"

"Got to keep those *Seven Seas* dry!"

With a wave, Jack took off running.

Jason had to see this. He positioned himself at the point of maximum drama: on the cliff toward the end of the first gorge, where he had an unobstructed view of the white water in the canyon and the whirlpool below.

The word had gone up and down the portage trail that a party was going to try the canyon. Everyone along the trail pressed to the edge of the cliff to see what would happen.

A shout came down from above: "They're on their way!"

Here came the *Yukon Belle* down the chute between the dark, narrow walls. Wiry Merritt Sloper, at the bow, was digging with a paddle. Fred Thompson and Jim Goodman sat side by side, each working an oar, while Jack stood at the stern, steering with the huge sweep. As the skiff raced through a succession of waves, Sloper's paddle often grabbed nothing but air as the bow was pitched high again and again. At a command from London, the two amidships suddenly pulled in their oars, and just in time—the skiff went flying downstream at breakneck speed, at one point no more than six feet from the wall.

When a sudden wave swept the big skiff sideways, London leaned on the sweep oar with all his might and pointed the bow downstream just in time to meet a huge curling wave that would surely have tipped them over. Sloper's paddle snapped in two under the force.

Once through that last wave of the first canyon, the *Yukon Belle* was shot headlong into the whirlpool. Once again, London braced the entire skiff against the violent water with his sweep and called for oars. Thompson and Goodman, facing the stern, had little idea where they were going, but the strength of their oars pulled the boat out of the whirlpool and headlong into the second canyon.

Cheers echoed all along the tops of the cliffs. "That man reads the water like a book," someone shouted.

Jack London had come up big.

## SIXTEEN

With Miles Canyon and the White Horse Rapids behind him, Jason paddled furiously north down the Yukon. The sun had lost its power, its arc now ominously low in the sky. No more calls from geese or swans, only from ravens, and the word they were croaking was *winter*.

It was do or die.

His canoe was fast, but he still had fifty miles of river before Lake Laberge, where the current would die on him for thirty miles.

"Pull!" he yelled. "Pull!"

Confused, the husky turned around in the bow of the canoe, seeming to ask what he wanted.

"Sorry, King! I meant me, not you!"

Suddenly King pricked up his wolflike ears and studied the shore. Jason stopped paddling, then heard a *chirrup* repeated several times.

There on the left, in the willows, was a cow moose, the first moose he'd ever seen.

From the shore downstream came deep grunts. A bull moose was attacking a small spruce tree and utterly demolishing it with its massive antlers. Suddenly the bull left off the attack, flared his nostrils, and proceeded upriver toward the female.

A second bull, hidden in the willows near the cow, charged out onto the river gravel to challenge the intruder. The bulls paused twenty feet from each other and lowered their antlers, pawing the ground and grunting battle cries. The giants were equally matched, and it was apparent there was going to be a fight. The current took the canoe around the bend before the bulls charged, but a moment later Jason heard the ringing collision of bone on bone.

The pale green Yukon was joined by the Takhini from the west, which briefly clouded it with silt. The valley opened up, and the cut banks disappeared as he entered a slow and swampy alder flat. Then, at the end of his second day below White Horse Rapids, the current died out altogether as he paddled into the head of windblown Lake Laberge.

The wind blew so fiercely that night, it seemed the spruces in his camp would surely snap. At last the gale died out in the hours before dawn. Jason woke to a sheet of ice stretching all the way to the barren highlands across the lake, and the fearful realization that he was trapped.

At dawn the trees were bending again, and, to his amazement, the ice broke into panes of glass that drifted and shattered before the wind. He didn't dare to take the time to warm himself with a fire, or to cook. The wind was blowing hard out of the northwest, and he had to get through this dead water and into the current before the ice returned to lock up the lake for good.

Jason hugged the west shore and paddled north, bundled like a polar bear from fur hat to sealskin mukluks, but without the clumsy mittens. His fingers felt like frozen claws. The windlashed surface of the lake was wild with waves and whitecaps, but as long as he hugged the shore, he could keep the canoe under control. Even so, the spray turned to ice in midair and fell tinkling into the canoe.

On his second day on the lake there were skiffs coming on from behind. On his third day, still hugging the shore, he couldn't see the skiffs over his shoulder anymore. He could guess the reason. With all their surface for the wind to catch, those boats would be kites; they'd end up wrecked on the far shore of the lake. All those people behind him were trapped in camp.

With each dawn the ice covering the lake was thicker than before, and each day it took longer for the wind to shatter and disperse it.

His fourth day on the lake, the squalls became so severe that he couldn't make any progress and had to go to shore. He was in a quandary. If he couldn't get off this lake, there would come the day, and very soon, when the morning ice covering Lake Laberge wouldn't break up at all. That would be the day that spelled disaster.

Out of desperation, he tried to see if King could pull the canoe from shore. Where the shoreline would allow it, it worked. With the dog straining at his utmost and Jason paddling like a berserker, they were able to keep going.

The sixth day dawned a dead calm. The ice on Laberge was an inch thick. What now? Wait until the ice was thick enough to walk on, then drag the canoe the rest of the way?

If he waited that long, the Yukon River beyond the lake would itself freeze over, and he'd be stranded with three hundred miles remaining.

Checkmate?

His antagonist, the wind, finally came to his aid. Late in the morning it blew hard enough to create a channel of open water along the western shore, and then it died out as suddenly as it had begun.

Here was his chance. Jason put the husky back in the bow and paddled north with all the strength he could muster. By twilight he was entering the narrowing outlet of the lake, and he felt the revival of the current. Before long it was rushing beneath him like floodwaters. There was just enough daylight remaining to allow him to see the illusion of the boulder-strewn river bottom rising up beneath him as the canoe poured with the slush ice into the reborn Yukon.

On the left shore, people. Behind them, cabins with sod roofs. An Indian village. He paddled for shore, half-dead from cold.

Arms motioned him in. "Plenty muck-a-muck," a man told him.

He was being invited to eat, he realized. All around the village, racks were full of drying salmon, but it was moose steaks they were roasting around their cook fires.

The Indians' dogs, all tied, were in an uproar at the sight of King, but no one paid any attention to their barking and leaping. People let him know he was fortunate to escape the lake. "*Tomolla*, no."

The next morning the Yukon narrowed into a winding, steep-walled canyon. He had to be careful not to hug the turns, where sweepers—trees undermined by the river but still clinging by their roots to the banks—sawed up and down in the current. In the tightest turn of all, he passed over an enormous submerged boulder that produced a vicious boil downstream. The boil caught the canoe, spun it suddenly, and King went flying into the river. It was all Jason could do to brace with his paddle and keep from capsizing.

"King!" he shouted, but the powerful husky was having no trouble keeping his head above the water. Jason made for a gravel beach as fast as he could, with King paddling close behind. The husky dragged himself on shore and shook himself out. They were back on the river minutes later.

It was a gray October day, with no help from the sun. The canoe passed the mouth of the Teslin River and a native village there. Now the Yukon was nearly twice as big as before. It snowed that night, three inches of snow as fine and dry as sugar.

The next day he passed the mouth of the Big Salmon River and another village.

On all sides, ice cakes were hissing in the Yukon. Shelves of ice were forming along the shore, extending ten and twenty feet out. As freeze-up lowered the level of the river, the ice shelves cracked noisily under their own weight and splashed into the water, adding even more ice to the rest jostling downstream.

He passed two more villages the following day at the mouth of the Little Salmon and the mouth of the Nordenskjold. The drying racks were full of salmon.

From around a bend in the river came the roar of rapids. Jason pulled the canoe onto the beach and walked above the sheer bank on the right side to take a look at what was making all the noise. Four stony islands scattered in a row across the Yukon divided its flow into five rushing channels. This had to be the Five Fingers, which his map noted as LAST RAPID.

The big waves in the central slots would surely spill him, but he could picture himself paddling the raceway closest to the eastern bank, where he stood.

Before he got back into the canoe he calmed himself by sitting for a few minutes with his companion. The best friend I ever hope to have, he mused. With the husky's winter coat fully grown out, including a creamy underfur, King looked more splendid and solid than ever.

"These Five Fingers can't stop us," Jason said to the husky. "Don't let anything stump you, King. That's what my father always said."

The husky, with a quick dart of his tongue, licked Jason's cheek.

"Five Fingers and an arm and a leg can't keep us from our pot of gold now, partner. We're a couple hundred miles—that's all we are—from staking our claim. We're going to be millionaires!"

Jason was sure he saw a grin on the husky's beautiful face. King barked once, twice.

"Yes, sir. We'll split everything down the middle. Fifty-fifty."

Back on the river, Jason yelled, "Watch our smoke!" at the top of his lungs, then paddled down the rightmost of the Five Fingers. He felt the sudden acceleration as the canoe dropped swiftly toward a train of foaming waves. The trick was to stay dead center and not let the swirling eddies on either side grab him.

The bow met the first wave head-on and rose high as it sliced cleanly through. Jason paddled hard, careful not to lose momentum, as the canoe dropped into a trough.

It rose with ice cakes on both sides onto a wave that broke over the bow and drenched him, all the way back at the stern, with icy spray. Steady!

Two more waves and they'd shot through. The rapids of the upper Yukon were all behind them. Jamie and her father came to mind; they'd paddled their canoe through this same rapid. Had they picked the same channel? Were they already working their claim, filling gunnysacks with nuggets?

Below Five Fingers the country opened up again, and the river meandered among dozens of islands, some half a mile or more in length. He stayed in the channel with the most current and the least ice. The bare bushes along the eastern shore were flecked with red.

Wild roses, he realized. Those red specks must be rose hips, the fruit Jamie had told him about, which would prevent scurvy. He knew a little about scurvy— the scourge of sailors, on account of their diet. It could make your teeth fall out. Scurvy could cripple you; it could even kill you.

Jason landed and went to take a look, then got a sack and started picking. He'd better take the time, he thought. Tomatoes and limes and such might not be available in Dawson City. A present for Abe and Ethan; he'd make tea drinkers of them.

He filled a sack, returned to the canoe and stowed it, then started on a second. This time he worked his way farther downstream and away from the river. He was finding rose hips almost half an inch in diameter. King was keeping an eye on him from a sunny clearing by the shore. It was a crisp day and the sky was a hard blue. Jason's breath made a cloud of frost every time he breathed out.

Suddenly he became aware of splashes of crimson in

the snow ahead. A few more steps, and he realized he was looking at a blood trail . . . and moose tracks. The blood looked fresh. Was it from a bull gored in a mating battle?

Here was a chance to present his brothers with a substantial amount of meat. With the rapids behind him, his canoe could float at least a hindquarter.

Jason quickly returned to the canoe for the rifle. "King," he called, and the husky ran to join him. At the moose trail, the husky's nose caught the scent of blood and the fur along his spine stood straight up.

The trail led no farther than a hundred yards, in and out of the alders and the willows. Suddenly, there was the moose, not forty feet in front of him, standing broadside in a small clearing, now turning its head to look at him. Six feet tall at the shoulders, no doubt, this bull was even more massive than the ones he'd seen earlier. The moose was bleeding from wounds on both sides of its neck and one behind the front shoulder.

Those were bullet holes, he realized, not antler wounds. Someone must be tracking the moose. An Indian? A Klondiker?

Jason turned around, saw no one. When he looked back, the moose was gone.

He followed the blood trail through the trees, more cautiously now, rifle at the ready. If he were to finish the moose, it would be a kindness to the animal and helpful to the hunter who was tracking it.

When he glimpsed the moose a few minutes later, it lay fallen in the snow, inert as stone. He wasn't going to have to shoot it after all.

Jason set the rifle against a tree and walked close. The antlers were so broad, he might not be able to touch from one side to the other with arms outspread.

Suddenly the moose blinked, and a hind leg twitched. It was still alive! Before Jason had time for a second thought, the moose was on its feet and charging.

No time to reach the rifle. Time only to run. He saw King look over his shoulder at the monster, saw the husky running too.

Jason tripped and went down hard. Instantly he was back up, but just then the bull rammed him from behind, its antlers like the cowcatcher on a locomotive. All at once the moose threw its rack up and back, and Jason went with the antlers high into the air and above the animal.

Involuntarily, his arms shot out to break his twisting fall and he grabbed hold of two antler tips. He'd landed belly-down in the broad, flat palms of the antlers. At once, the moose was trying to shake him off, and might have. He wrapped his legs around the moose's long, tapering head and clung with all his strength.

Hang on, he told himself. If he shakes me loose, then gores me or kicks me, I'm dead.

He could hear King barking. He could see the blur of the husky darting in and out.

The moose started ramming its head into the ground, trying to smash Jason into the ground. He held on. Suddenly the beast buckled underneath him, and Jason's knees hit the earth. His legs had lost their hold; all he had now was the grip of his hands on the antler tines. He dared not let go.

King rushed in and tried to get under the animal's throat. The moose stood up suddenly, kicking at the husky with its front hooves. King backed away, and the moose tried to shake Jason loose with wild gyrations of its head, and then to crush him into the ground.

Jason felt his legs taking a beating. The strength had

gone out of his arms; he doubted he could hold on any longer. He slipped, and found himself looking directly into the animal's eyes. The smell of musk and blood was bestial. The monster was making an incongruous cooing sound.

The moose buckled to its knees once again, ramming Jason back to the earth. The animal was utterly exhausted, and so was he.

As the moose's front legs kicked forward in yet another attempt to stand, Jason felt a hoof pin one of his boots to the ground. The weight on his foot and the sudden pulling back of the monster's antlers finally ripped his hands from their grip, and he was knocked loose.

Quicker than thought, he saw the enormous forelegs raining down, and shielded his face. His arms and chest took a terrible trampling from the front hooves.

Though the wind was knocked out of him, he managed to roll over as the moose momentarily turned to face King, who was barking in a frenzy. Then he was being trampled again, this time all over his back and legs.

Jason looked over his shoulder. The moose had its head down, about to gore him with those sharp tines, when the husky came flying. The moose turned its antlers toward the dog instead, and flung King aside like a rag doll.

A moment later the hooves rained down again, a shot rang out, and then all was darkness.

## SEVENTEEN

When Jason came to, he knew only pain. At first he was aware of a sharp stab in his chest with the intake of even the slightest breath, but then he felt pain from head to toe and deep inside.

He opened his eyes. Everything was dim and murky. The only light was coming from a crude window made from pieces of bottles stuck in hardened mud. He was in a cabin, he realized. Outside, it was snowing.

He could hear a fire crackling in a stove, but he couldn't turn his head to see the stove. The pain from throughout his body seemed to rush all at once to the back of his head. Suddenly he remembered the moose, and then he remembered the dog flung through the air off its enormous antlers. Was King alive?

Jason lapsed into darkness again, and when he woke, it was to the husky's face only inches from his. "King," he said, "King."

126

The husky nuzzled his cheek.

"You're still alive." He reached to stroke the husky's head, but the movement hurt too much and he had to pull back. The dog, satisfied that Jason was alive, lay down by the stove with a series of yelps.

Both were hurt bad, but both were alive. Where was this cabin? Who had brought him here?

Jason slept.

The next time he woke, it was to candlelight and the shadow of a man moving in the room. The shadow came and went during the hazy, slow passage of time. The specter was tall and lean, with piercing dark eyes under knitted brows and a wide-brimmed prospector's hat. His face was gaunt, brooding, chiseled from solid granite, it seemed.

"Where am I?" Jason managed. "Dawson City?"

"Hardly," the man grunted. "You're a couple of miles below Five Fingers. Dawson is two hundred and fifty miles downriver."

Jason tried to think, to remember. "I have to get going," he said. "I have to get to Dawson City before the river freezes up." With the breath it took to speak, his ribs felt like a knife was twisting in them.

The man shook his head doubtfully. "The year before last, I fell onto a broken-off tree branch. It went through my leg like a spear. I had to be somewhere too, but I couldn't even stand up for two weeks. So don't tell me you have to get to Dawson City. Winter's going to have the last word on that. Are you by yourself?"

Jason nodded, struggling against his confusion. "I still don't understand how I—why I'm not dead, and where you came from. Did you fire the shot?"

"I'd been trying to catch up with that moose all morning. I heard some commotion and was coming up real careful. As I caught sight of you, that bull was within an instant of punching you full of holes, but your dog came leaping in. In the time it took me to raise my rifle and shoot, the dog went flying and the moose had gone back to giving you the devil with his hooves. How did you let that happen? Set your rifle down and walked up on the animal, thinking it was dead?"

It was all coming back. Jason groaned in agreement.

"That's enough talk. You're in worse shape than you know. You've been out cold for twenty-four hours."

The darkness swept back in on him, and he slept.

In the morning Jason was able to move enough to clean himself with a bucket of hot water the man had heated on the stove. His entire body was black-and-blue. Every movement brought a whirlwind of pain. The back of his head had a fist-sized lump that pounded relentlessly with every beat of his heart.

"Where's it hurt worst?" came the man's voice.

"Ribs. I think I have some cracked ribs."

It kept snowing, and the sky stayed dark. Before the sun failed, Jason was able to go to the open door, though every step hurt, and look out. King got up, whimpering, and looked out with him. The cabin was situated at the mouth of a creek about fifty yards back from the Yukon. The Yukon's opposite shore was dominated by a barren bluff, pure white with snow.

The shelves of ice along the banks had grown toward the center of the river, nearly closing the open channel. "I hope you're heading to Dawson and can take me along," Jason said over his shoulder.

"I'm heading the other direction, and I'm in a hurry. I'm aiming to trade my canoe for a sled at the village at the mouth of the Nordenskjold."

"And get some dogs to pull your sled?"

"I pull my own sled."

It made no sense that a prospector would be going away from Dawson City instead of toward it, but Jason wasn't going to point that out. "I'm worried about my canoe," he said.

"I pulled it onto high ground. All the grub from your outfit is up in the cache where the critters can't get it, even your rose fruit. I brought enough grub inside, you won't have to climb until you're able—the ladder's around back. You got nothing to worry about."

Easy for you to say, Jason thought. He craned his neck out the door and spotted the cache high in the air on four stilts. Suddenly, it hurt too much to stand. He had to go lie down on the bunk.

King got up from beside the stove and lay down close to him. Jason dangled an arm over the side of the bunk and found the husky's head. Momentarily, Jason was soothed. Everything would be all right. Still, he kept trying to picture what was going to come of his setback. He might be alive, but he was in bad trouble with ice growing on the river by the minute. What was he going to do?

The prospector went outside, then returned a few minutes later with a slab of meat. He fried some steaks, made bannock and coffee. His dark, full mustache turned down at the corners of his face, which was cheerless as the landscape outside. "Sure glad I was close to your cabin," Jason said with forced enthusiasm as he chewed carefully. Even eating hurt.

The man gave a contemptuous glance around the room. "Ain't my cabin. I wouldn't have set foot in here if you hadn't needed a place to get out of the weather."

"Couldn't I just drift down to Dawson City in my canoe?"

"You don't understand. The river can freeze up uncannily sudden—slabs of ice tearing every which way. I've seen it bust a steamboat into matchsticks. You've got a cabin here with a stove in it. Count yourself lucky. A lot of cheechakos are going to die this winter. Hunker down, play it safe, ride out the winter. You have a rifle and ammunition. One moose and you'd be in good shape."

"Stay here until breakup? Right here? You don't understand. . . . I have two brothers in Dawson City."

"Yeah, and I got a wife and three kids in Colorado. Try it if you dare; I'm not going to be here to stop you. There's lots of ways to die in the North. Simply getting your feet wet when it's cold can kill you. How long have your brothers been in Dawson?"

"Three weeks, maybe. They must've staked by now. I was hoping to stake before winter myself."

"Dawson is a fool's paradise," the prospector said bitterly.

"So where are you heading with your sled?"

"Upriver to the Little Salmon, then cross-country northeast to the headwaters of the Stewart."

"Did you come over the Chilkoot?"

"About three years ago I did. Going to strike it rich, are you?"

"Aim to."

"They say there's quite a few coming over the Chilkoot, making ready to come downriver with the breakup next spring."

"Thousands and thousands. I guess tens of thousands if you count everyone pouring into Dyea and Skagway. . . . My name's Jason Hawthorn. I thank you for helping me out."

The man shrugged. "The Golden Rule is the code of the Yukon Order of Pioneers, or at least it used to be. 'Do unto others as you would be done by.'"

The bitterness in the man's voice was unmistakable. Jason asked his name.

"Robert Henderson. Just call me Henderson. Heard my name before?"

Jason wagged his head. "Should I have?"

The man smiled sardonically. It was the first smile Jason had seen from him. "No, no . . . I'm a ghost. I've become a ghost."

Jason was baffled, and a little unnerved. "This moose we're eating . . . this must be the one I got tangled up with?"

"Must've weighed fifteen hundred pounds. All I brought back was a hindquarter. By the time I went for more, a bear had gotten to it—dragged the rest of the carcass a short ways, then covered it with duff and branches. Figured I'd leave it there, fouled as it was. No doubt that bear's fixin' to den and not much interested in eating. In the spring, though, when it comes out, it'll remember where it cached the meat. The den is probably close by. Too bad I didn't spot it."

"Why is that?"

"For future reference. This was a black bear—I saw a print—and black bears are good eating. The Indians keep close track of den sites. In winter, they'll hunt the bear in its den."

"Really? In its den?"

"That shouldn't sound so amazing. I mean, the bear is asleep."

"Have you ever done that?"

"Never had the occasion."

Though Henderson said he was going to go, and

soon, Jason didn't really believe it. How could Henderson leave him there, alone?

And yet, in the morning, Henderson did just that. Packed his things, said good-bye and good luck, and ghosted away. Jason fought the impulse to call him back, to cajole, to beg, but he kept his tongue as fear crept into him as tangibly as the cold. Henderson headed upriver, paddling and then poling.

Jason tried to put the gaunt, tortured prospector out of his thoughts. He stared downriver at the bleak skeletal cottonwoods, his mind lurching to plot his escape. He'd come too far for this to happen to him.

Downstream, the Yukon broke into channels as it wound its way among numerous islands. Two hundred and fifty miles, no rapids. Henderson was wrong about having to stay here. Why couldn't he just wrap himself in his blankets and float?

Because it wasn't only the matter of not being able to paddle. He couldn't make camp, split wood, make a fire, or cook.

In a few weeks' time he would be able to do those things. The cabin was warm, and he needed to heal.

A few weeks would be too late.

How could Henderson have left him? He was only a cheechako. He might not even have the grub to get through the winter. People said breakup came at the end of May. That was seven months away!

At least Henderson had left him with a supply of split firewood, enough for a few weeks, it looked like. And as he looked around he realized that Henderson had left a small crosscut saw as well as a pair of snowshoes—five-foot long Indian-made snowshoes of birch frames and rawhide to keep him above the snow when he was out looking for that moose or getting firewood.

No, he had no bone to pick with Henderson. The man had saved his life.

What about Jack London? If Jack hadn't given him the outfit, he would've stayed on the ocean side of the Chilkoot pass, maybe even gone home.

What about his brothers? They were sitting pretty in Dawson only because they'd taken his inheritance for packing money.

Then there was Jamie, that pretty girl, telling him to collect rose hips. He would never have run into that moose if it hadn't been for her.

He laughed out loud, at himself. It was a bitter laugh born of desperation, and it hurt.

He had only himself to blame.


As the days passed, Jason fought the impulse to throw himself in the canoe and drift. A hundred times he told himself that Henderson was wrong. The moon was up; he could drift around the clock bundled in his blankets, all the way to the Golden City.

But he kept picturing the ice pitching up all around him and the canoe being ground to matchsticks. He stayed where he was, immobilized. His ribs were barely improved, and he was still a mass of bruises. He kept looking upstream for straggling Klondikers who might take him down to Dawson.

None came. Ravens and gray jays were the only living things in the country, it seemed, besides him and the dog and the wolves in the distance. Their howling seemed to drive a cold nail deeper into his heart with each passing day.

As the days and his spirits darkened, he watched the

surface of the river freeze from shore to shore. Very suddenly at the last, just as Henderson had predicted, the jagged, grinding shapes pitched up and locked into place with a crash of finality.

Winter.

## EIGHTEEN

The sound of a gunshot, close by, exploded the oppressive silence. The husky came instantly to his feet, ears at the alert. With King at his side, Jason hobbled outside the cabin to investigate, but there was no one around. He hollered himself hoarse. No one was there. The hair on the back of his neck rose; he was scared down to the roots of his chattering teeth.

The oppressive, almost palpable silence closed back in. Winter abhorred sound. There was only the emptiness of the vast northern forest.

The next day, two more gunshots, almost certainly coming from the cottonwoods along the creek. Again, silence, and no tracks in the snow. No one had been there.

It must be the trees themselves, Jason realized, bursting and splitting in the extreme cold.

He used to pride himself on being able to go it alone, to shake off his bouts of loneliness. No longer. Thank God for King. This place would have already made him crazy with terror if it weren't for the husky.

In the mornings, every nailhead on the inside of the cabin was covered with hoarfrost. It took time for the little sheet-iron stove to push back the cold. One day, behind the cabin, he discovered a rusty thermometer nailed to a spruce tree. Midday the mercury was registering twenty-five degrees below zero.

He had to spend hours outside now, making firewood, though every swing of the ax reverberated in his ribs. And he had to keep open the hole in the creek where Henderson had been drawing water with the bucket.

The husky was always eager to go out, bite the snow, roll in it. Jason was still awed by the bitter cold, even though he bundled himself thick as a bear to go out. He'd never known what cold was before, not really. Here in the North it seemed an element all its own, a pervasive and lethal liquid pouring down out of the sky. Though he was getting by from one day to the next, the idea of wintering here was incomprehensible.

On the last day of October, according to the nicks he was carving on the cabin wall, he thought he heard voices from downriver.

He told himself that the voices were coming from the dark corners of his imagination.

He heard them again. Shouts. People shouting, and this time not far away.

You've lost your mind, he told himself.

But King was growling.

Jason started to get up. King began barking.

Suddenly the door shook with loud blows.

Abruptly, the door was pulled open. There stood a man with cracked lips, a frostbitten white patch at the tip of his nose, icicles in his mustache, and eyes wide like a refugee from an asylum. As the man lowered his heavy pack to the ground and bent to unbuckle his snowshoes, he stammered something about the cabin.

Was this the owner of the cabin, come to claim it?

Seven or eight more men under heavy burdens were trudging toward the cabin, mechanically, like sleepwalkers. The last was pulling someone on a sled, someone propped up against a packsack.

Would they demand that he give up the cabin?

With a glance back toward the figure on the sled, the man at the door barked, "Get him inside."

It was a boy on the sled, a boy no older than twelve. He tried to look past Jason into the cabin. The boy's face was a mask of fright, as if he was being led to his execution.

Four men struggled to carry the boy inside. "Watch that foot!" one of them cried out, too late, as the boy's right foot, wrapped in a blanket, bumped against the door frame. Jason expected the boy to howl in pain, but there came no reaction at all. The blanket fell away, revealing a foot and lower leg massively swollen and covered with only a heavy sock.

Jason looked to their leader for an explanation.

"Do you have any whiskey?" the man demanded. His eyes were jittery and his voice brittle as glass.

Jason shook his head.

"It probably wouldn't do much good anyway. Lay Charlie down on the floor there—right here on the middle of the floor where we can hold him down."

"For the love of God, Uncle George!" the boy cried.

"Who's going to do it?" The boy's uncle was looking wildly around the room at the faces of the men who'd crowded into the cabin. All eyes were averted as they stamped their feet and pushed to get close to the warmth of the stove.

"Henry, you're a blacksmith."

"Aye, a blacksmith, not a butcher."

"He's your nephew, Maguire," another man growled.

"It will heal, Uncle George!" the boy begged. "Give it time!"

The boy's uncle knelt and began to unroll the large wool sock. A cloying stench wafted across the room and nearly knocked Jason down.

Men cursed and reached for bandannas or handkerchiefs, which they pressed to their mouths and noses. All eyes fell on the dead limb, and the room was filled with revulsion. The boy's right foot and lower leg were horribly distended and blackened with rotting tissue. The boy himself, on seeing it, shrank in horror and wailed, "No! No!"

The word *gangrene* was spoken, and Jason heard another voice whisper, "The poison's probably spread already."

Maguire stoked the stove full from the pile of kindling there, then opened the draft slot wide. The kindling caught with a roar, and within minutes the thin walls of the stove were glowing bright red. "Whose knife is razor sharp?" he demanded.

A man with a walrus mustache produced a broad bowie knife from the scabbard at his hip.

"Maybe you should use this saw," another man put in, indicating the crosscut saw that Henderson had left behind.

"Give me both, then. That pail of water, let's put it on to boil."

The boy's eyes, as he lay splayed out on the floor, seemed to have rolled back into his skull. He was deathly pale, and his chest was heaving with fright.

His uncle's eyes were searching the room. They came to rest on a short-handled shovel hanging from the cabin wall. "Stick the blade of the shovel into the stove, Henry. I'll need it red-hot."

"What for?"

"To seal the stump so he doesn't bleed to death. Give me that stick there, Johnson, for between his teeth, so he doesn't bite his tongue off. Don't any of you leave; I want all of you here to help hold him down."

Jason wiped his forehead. He'd broken out in a cold sweat. Quickly, he pulled on his mackinaw and the oilskin overcoat, put on his fur hat and mittens, and backed out the door.

Outside, Jason reeled away from the cabin, wading in the knee-deep snow, with the husky following behind. He had to get away. He walked upstream toward the Five Fingers, along the windward side of the Yukon's bank, where the snow was crusted stiff. When he thought he'd gone far enough that he wouldn't possibly hear, he crumpled in the snow and held the dog close.

The first scream carried far in the extreme cold, and Jason heard it distinctly, all the more horrible for the distance it had traveled. Though Jason clapped his mittens to his ears, he continued to hear the boy's torment, worse than he'd ever imagined from souls cast into hell.

The husky too recoiled from the sound of the screams—at first his ears lay down flat, then he yawned anxiously, and then he whimpered. Jason broke into tears. He'd heard about battlefield surgery during the

Civil War. Once he'd asked his father how men could have endured it. His father had answered laconically, "They had no choice."

After a minute the forest and the undulating frozen field of white that was the river were again swathed with the eerie silence of winter. Had the boy blacked out? Had he bled to death? For long minutes Jason stayed where he was, dreading to return. Yet he had to find out what the men intended to do. If it was their cabin, or if they were moving in regardless, he was in bad trouble.

To Jason's surprise as he neared the cabin, the men were already under way, bent under their heavy pack-sacks and moving upriver fast in their snowshoes. The boy's uncle, rifle across his chest, was in the lead, as before. The sled and the boy were nowhere to be seen.

Jason stood in their path. As they approached and halted in front of him, he sputtered, "Is he dead, then?"

"Alive, but he lost a lot of blood," the boy's wild-eyed uncle explained. "Out cold. He'll likely die."

"You're leaving without him?"

"We have no choice! We can't wait him out."

"But where are you going? Where did you come from?"

The man's eyes blazed with panicky fire. "We've no time for talk and explanations. Lost too much time already."

"You can't leave him behind!"

"We have no choice," Maguire repeated. "It was Charlie's bad luck he froze his foot, and there's nothing can undo that."

"You can't leave him!"

The man brandished his rifle. "Get out of my way!"

"You don't understand—I don't have the grub to feed

myself. What have you left me to feed him with, if he lives?"

The man's face went apoplectic with fury. He brandished the rifle again; King growled deep in his throat.

"Don't *you* understand?" Maguire cried. "We have nothing to give you. We have only what's on our backs, with two hundred and fifty miles to go and every day shorter than the last. Now, move aside or I'll shoot you where you stand. Put him out in the cold if you must!"

Jason hesitated, scarcely believing what he'd just heard. Then he stepped aside.

None of them, as they passed by, would look him in the eye. In shame, they trudged mechanically upriver like the walking dead.

## NINETEEN

In a fever-tossed delirium, the boy named Charlie teetered along the razor-thin margin between life and death. In and out of consciousness, he fought Jason's attempts to force tea and oatmeal and stewed fruit down him, to change his dressing and salve his wound, to bathe him clean when he fouled himself. Yet Jason prevailed, and kept him alive.

Three, four, five, six days. There were times when Jason thought he couldn't bear the boy's torment another minute.

"Put him out in the cold," his uncle had said. Let the cold kill him. Put him out of his misery the way horses were put out of their misery on the Dead Horse Trail.

What if Henderson had done the same to him?

Monstrous, even to think of it. He had to fight to keep

this tangle-haired kid alive, no matter what might come of it—even if it meant starvation for both of them.

When the fever broke at last and the boy's eyes came into focus, his gaze darted wildly around the cabin from Jason to the husky to the door, then back to Jason. "Who are you?"

"Jason Hawthorn."

"Where are they? I'll never catch up!"

He doesn't remember about his leg, Jason realized. He doesn't know. "They're long gone," Jason said. "You weren't well enough to travel."

The boy's eyes went around the room, from the opposite bunk and the shelf of magazines above it, to the wash on the clothesline strung across the room, to the window made of bottles. "Who else lives here?"

"Just me. I'm holing up here for the winter, on the way to finding my brothers in Dawson City."

"Is that . . . a wolf?"

"It's a dog. A husky. His name's King."

At the mention of his name, King got up and went to the boy's side, let himself be petted.

"It's warm in here," the boy said approvingly.

"That's right. Nice and warm. Try to rest."

Shortly after he awoke the next time, the boy looked startled. His head snapped back with a sudden realization, as if he'd taken a punch. Very slowly, he lifted the blanket, and he gasped.

Then he stared at the floor and saw the enormous darkened bloodstain there. Jason had tried without success to wash it away. The boy's face went pale as a corpse and his lips began to tremble.

Try to take his mind off the leg, Jason thought. "Where were they going, Charlie?"

"Who?"

"Your uncle, and the others. Where were they going?"

"Skagway," the boy mumbled.

He's still delirious, Jason thought. Try it another way. "Where did you start out from?"

With an absent look came the answer: "Chicago." With that, the dark-haired boy groaned and looked away, buried his face in the blanket, and sobbed himself to sleep.

Jason went outside to split wood and to think. If only he knew what to do, how to help this boy cope with the calamity that had come crashing down on him. Make some kind of crutches? If the boy was going to be able to get around at all, he'd need them. Fashioning crutches would give Jason something to do. And it would keep his mind off his biggest worry, whether he had enough food to take the two of them through the winter. Henderson had said he should get a moose, but there hadn't been a moose around since the one that nearly killed him.

On the ridge above the creek, Jason found young birches of just the right diameter for crutches. The snowshoe frames were made of birch, and so were canoe paddles and sleds. Birch should be good for crutches as well. While he was among the birches, he would strip more bark for fire starter.

Jason was back in the cabin whittling lengths for the crutches when the boy wakened again. "I have to go outside," Charlie said.

As the boy tried to stand on his left leg, he swooned and fell back to the bunk.

"You lost enough blood for two people. Don't try getting up just yet."

The boy stared at him fiercely. "Just help me up, will you? Don't tell me not to try."

Jason hesitated, then stepped closer. Charlie tried again, clutching tight this time, and managed to hop outside, where he leaned on the cabin and relieved himself.

"Does it hurt bad?" Jason asked afterward. He didn't want to say the word *stump*.

"Hurts worse when I stand up."

After he finished helping Charlie back to his bunk, Jason went outside. It was late afternoon already, time to think about supper. He took the ladder from behind the cabin and climbed up to the cache. He threw the makings for a mulligan stew into a bag—some bacon, dried onions, dried potatoes, and other dried soup vegetables.

In the cabin, he spread it all out on the table, then started heating water in a stewpot on top of the stove. Charlie was awake, lying on the bunk with his hands behind his head, staring at the log rafters.

"This will need to soak and simmer for a while," Jason said, tossing the vegetables into the water. "I'll fry up the bacon a little later."

"Can I stay here?" Charlie asked, his eyes fixed on the ceiling.

Jason threw some salt in the pot, then covered it. "I could use the company."

"Good," the boy whispered. Then he turned to face Jason, propping himself on his left elbow. "How long were they here?"

"Your uncle and the rest? Not long. They thought you were a goner."

"When they get back home to Chicago, that's what they'll tell my mother. They'll tell her I'm dead."

"Well then, you'll just have to surprise her."

A faint smile crossed Charlie's face. "She'd like that, all right," he agreed, nodding his head. But the smile was erased almost immediately by dread.

Jason wished the boy would talk. He wanted to hear his story. "Tell me again, Charlie, where your uncle and the others were going, and where you started from."

"We were trying to get to Skagway. We started in Dawson City."

"You've been to Dawson?" Jason could barely believe what he was hearing. "How long were you there?"

"Ten days or so. We got there the twenty-fifth of September."

"You might have seen my brothers," Jason said urgently. "Their names are Abe and Ethan. They're twenty-three and twenty-one. Abraham's taller, with a mustache; Ethan's powerful like a lumberjack and has a beard."

Charlie put his right hand to the tousled hair spilling over his forehead, pulled on it as he closed his eyes. "I don't remember those names," he said at last. "So many people there. Everyone has a mustache or a beard."

"I suppose they were already at the creeks, staking a claim. Did you?"

"Stake a claim? No, we didn't. People were saying that the new discoveries don't amount to much. It looks like maybe you had to be there earlier, maybe a lot earlier."

"But you *did* get there early, and so did my brothers. The Klondike is the richest goldfield in the world!"

"I suppose so, but how big? Oh, lots of people still think there will be new strikes anytime now—maybe they're right. I'm sorry; I just said what I heard."

Jason's mind was reeling. It can't be too late, he thought; it just can't be.

"There'll be new strikes," Jason insisted. "There have to be."

"Gold wasn't even what people were talking about. Famine, that's what everybody was talking about. There's hardly any food there."

Jason winced. "My brothers traded away some of their grub."

"We never had much, and that's why we had to turn around. We had money, because of the investors at the bank where my uncle's a clerk. All the way from Chicago, my uncle kept saying, 'We can buy grub in Dawson. The most important thing is to go fast and get there first.' When we got to customs, the Mounties weren't enforcing the weight limit for food yet—"

"They are now. How many people are there in Dawson City?"

"They say three or four thousand have been there almost since the beginning—August a year ago. When we got there, everybody was waiting for five steamboats that were supposed to be bringing supplies upriver all the way from the ocean. Two different companies in Dawson have food warehouses—both guarded by men with rifles—but there's hardly any food to buy. A couple pounds of beans or flour was all they'd sell you."

Jason could still hardly believe Charlie had been to Dawson City, had just come from there. "Did you see any gold?" he asked, hoping Charlie wouldn't tire soon and leave off telling what he knew.

"I sure did. A man buys a shovel, he puts down dust or nuggets. People had gold, all right. Everybody was saying that the grub was going to sell out fast, though, once the steamboats arrived, so we stayed close. Everyone in town was listening for a whistle and keeping one eye on the river. But only two steamboats ever got through, and by the time they did, the ice was thirty feet out from the shore."

"Did you buy food then?"

"No. They hardly had any once they got to Dawson. Way downriver the boats got stuck on sandbars, because of the low water. They had to unload half their cargo to get unstuck; then the other half got robbed at some Alaska mining camp. About all they had left when they got to Dawson was hardware."

"Good Lord!"

"You should've seen the panic." Charlie was sitting up on his bunk now, his eyes wild, as if he were seeing it all again. "The inspector in charge of the Mounties posted a notice on Front Street, right by the river. It said something like 'For those who have not laid in a winter's supply, to remain longer in Dawson City is to court death by starvation, or at least the certainty of sickness from scurvy and other troubles. Starvation now stares everyone in the face who is hoping and waiting for outside relief.'"

"My brothers . . ."

"It was bedlam. An official from one of the trading companies went running up and down Front Street yelling, 'Go! Go! Flee for your lives! There is no time to lose! There are some supplies down at Fort Yukon. Whichever way you go, up the river or down, it's hazardous—but you must make the try!'"

Suddenly Jason was struck with a sickening realization. His brothers might not even *be* in Dawson. They might have gone downriver!

"What did people do?" he asked. "Did many leave?"

"At least fifty small boats took off within an hour, to be the first ones to Fort Yukon, which is more than three hundred miles downstream. At the same time, there was an official from another trading company who was calling the other fellow a frightened little cheechako. He said there wouldn't be enough food down at Fort Yukon to feed everybody who was evacuating Dawson City. 'Stay put in Dawson,' he said. 'There will be no starvation. If there is starvation, it won't be until spring.'"

Jason couldn't help laughing. "That must have sounded reassuring."

"Everyone was crazy trying to make up their minds. The two steamboats were leaving within hours to try to beat the ice down to Fort Yukon. Some people were saying it was too late; the ice was going to catch them and wreck the boats, and they'd be stranded. Still, the decks of those two boats were full to bursting, and we kept wondering down to the last minute if we should get on board."

"Why didn't you?"

"My uncle George had been running around like a chicken with its head cut off. He'd found a decrepit little steamboat called the *Kieukik*, and he'd got it in his mind that the only safe thing to do was to backtrack the way we'd come, and hike back over the Chilkoot Pass. So that's what we did—started back upriver—but the machinery on the boat kept breaking down. A week later we'd gone only thirty-five miles."

"Battling the ice, I bet."

"You're right; there was ice on all sides. Finally we ripped a gash in the hull and set out in Indian canoes. We thought we'd be able to buy some more food at the mouth of the Stewart River—we knew that some Klondikers had built winter cabins on the islands in the

Yukon there. But they weren't willing to sell more than a few pounds from their outfits—they were worried about famine too.

"By this time the river froze up, and we had to abandon the canoes and go on foot. A week or so later—I don't remember exactly; it was all a nightmare—my right leg went through the ice and my boot filled with water. I was walking at the end of the line. I didn't tell anybody it had happened, because my uncle—everybody, really—was crazy to keep going. My uncle was always yelling at me to keep up, like it was all my fault. I was in a daze and I just kept walking.

"In camp I was so exhausted, I didn't even pull my boot off to dry it out. We built two big bonfires and slept real close to the fire, as usual. I thought, with my boot close to the fire, I'd be fine. I felt no pain. Sometime during the night, in my sleep, I must have shifted position, and my foot ended up nowhere close to the fire. My sock and my boot were still wet, and my foot froze. That's how it happened." With this, Charlie fell silent.

Jason started frying up the bacon for the stew. Then he reached over and handed the boy a piece of yeast cake. "Here. You can chew on this until the stew's ready."

Charlie took the food. His face had paled and he looked exhausted. "Thanks—I'm starving. How long can I stay here?"

"Until we float out together in the spring, unless you feel like hiking over the Chilkoot this winter. Don't think I'd join you. . . ."

The boy had eaten only a mouthful when he looked up with a sudden question on his face. "What about grub? Do we have enough?"

Instantly, Jason knew he had to steer a path around

the truth. This boy wasn't strong enough to hear it, at least not anytime soon. He knew Charlie couldn't possibly climb up to the cache to discover their true predicament. "We're okay if we pace ourselves," Jason answered, doing his best to sound convincing. "Otherwise, I wouldn't have told them to leave you here with me."

The next day Jason went searching for the carcass of the moose that had almost killed him, the one Henderson said a black bear had eaten from and covered up for the spring. Right now it wouldn't bother him in the least that the bear had eaten from it if he could claim the rest.

King's nose found the carcass, or what was left of it. Wolves had been there, wolves and ravens. Nothing remained but the bones.

Bad luck. More bad luck.

He'd had enough. Nothing was turning out like he'd thought.

"A lot of cheechakos will die this winter," Henderson had said.

Jason found himself shaking, and not from the cold.

## TWENTY

Mostly there was twilight, with shades of lavender along the skyline where the November sun was hiding. Some days Jason felled dead trees and sawed them into lengths for King to sled to the cabin for firewood. Most days he took the rifle and went hunting.

Midmorning, the sun would rise pale and weak. It barely climbed above the hills to the south, upriver. During its low three-hour run, the light was golden and glowing, like a continual sunset. The snow was three feet deep, four where the trees kept it from blowing.

Upstream and downstream, with King at his side, Jason snowshoed back and forth across the frozen river. The ice was windblown and hard as iron. With slow, deliberate steps and rifle at the ready, he stalked the breaks and the thickets, hair-triggered with anticipation but sensing there was nothing to hunt. He would pause for long minutes, trying to glean the faintest movement from the landscape, but the world seemed to have gone empty.

Why wasn't he seeing any moose? Henderson had made it sound so easy. Had Henderson ever wintered here? Did he know for a fact that the moose wintered here?

Nothing came easy. Everything seemed to be working against him. Charlie, after the torrent of talk at first, had frozen up like the Yukon. Whatever currents were stirring underneath the blank mask that was his face, Jason could only guess. Anger at his uncle must be one of them, anger at himself for letting his foot freeze might be another, but the strongest current had to be hopelessness at his one-legged future. The hurt behind his voice seemed to say that no one who had both legs had any right to speak on the subject.

He'd tried cheering Charlie up a dozen different ways; Charlie would have none of them. After the first few days, Charlie wouldn't even meet his eyes. The boy's only consolation seemed to be the deck of cards he'd pulled out of his packsack. The only game he would play was solitaire.

No, Charlie had one other consolation: King. In the evenings, one hand would turn over the cards while the other rested on the husky.

Every day, when Jason was farthest from the cabin, he'd find himself puzzling over the problem of Charlie. More and more, it was making *him* angry. It was like trying to tread water in a storm-tossed ocean with an anchor chained to his foot.

Charlie wouldn't even learn to use the crutches! There was no excuse for that. Granted that the cabin was small, and he could get around by leaning on things and hopping, but that was no excuse. He wasn't going to be able to hop through the rest of his life. Didn't he see that?

Then Jason would force his mind off Charlie and look around at the frozen mountains. It was still so strange to find himself in this place, to hear the sound of his own breathing in the midst of the emptiness, to see his breath and the dog's crystallize in the air. It was strange the way the ice fog would come and go, and it was strange returning to the cabin sometimes and seeing the flue smoke bent down to the ground by the cold.

Then came the day no smoke at all was coming from the cabin. It was King who stopped in his tracks and swiveled his ears forward, recognizing that something was amiss. What was it? Why had the fire gone out?

With deep foreboding, Jason snowshoed hurriedly up to the cabin door. He fought back his fears, burst through the door, and found Charlie sitting at the little table, playing solitaire in the cold.

"What happened?" he demanded

"Nothing," Charlie answered flatly, staring at the cards. He had his coat and his fur hat on, and every breath was making a cloud in the room, it was so cold.

Jason's eyes went to the heap of kindling and split firewood of various sizes—all unburned, none of it used since morning. "You let the fire go out," Jason said, his voice loaded with tension. "Why?"

Charlie shrugged. "Saving wood."

Jason wanted to scream at him, wanted to knock over the little table, scatter the cards all over the floor. He couldn't take much more of this. "What are you talking about?" he demanded. "You know we have plenty of wood—I told you that."

"You told me everything."

"What do you mean by that?"

"You have a better way to do everything—to start a fire, to keep it burning. . . . Now I've let it go out. I can't do anything right."

Charlie's lip was trembling. King was looking at him with great concern.

Jason was struck by the husky's reaction, humbled by it. He felt his own anger begin to ebb away. This kid was only twelve years old, and he was scared. Jason pulled up the other chair, sat down close to Charlie. He didn't know what he was going to do or say, but he had to do something. He reached for Charlie's hand as Charlie was turning over a card, held it firm. "Charlie," he said, "I can't do this alone."

"Oh yes you could. You'd be a lot better off without me."

"That's not true, Charlie. I need you."

"For what? You do everything. You cook, you clean up, you start the fire, you split the wood, you get the moose—"

"You see a moose?" Jason quipped, hoping to lighten the mood.

"You won't let me do anything. You do it all."

"Won't *let* you? Hey, wait a minute, this sounds like a conversation I used to have with my oldest brother, only now I'm on the other side. Go ahead, start the fire, make supper. . . ."

"I could split wood too, you know."

Jason was about to express his doubts. Suddenly he knew the right thing to say, and he even believed it to be true. "I'm sure you can do whatever you set your mind to."

With that, the thunderstorm in Charlie's head seemed to break. He started the fire and set about making a stew.

They shared the meal with quiet satisfaction. After dinner, they played cards together—three-card monte. Charlie was looking him in the eye now. Jason realized he liked this kid, really liked him.

What else could he do, he wondered, to help Charlie get back in the game?

"I've been thinking about the hunting," Jason said. "Maybe the moose can detect King's scent. Starting tomorrow, I'm going to leave him here. If I get something, then he can still sled the meat."

"I'll teach him to play three-card monte," Charlie said, a smile lighting his long-blank face.

In the morning the wind was howling, and snow was blowing horizontally. This wasn't a day for hunting. Jason decided to read a little, then drifted off to sleep.

He awoke midday, to find the husky at his side but Charlie gone. He had the sudden premonition that something had happened to him, and he craned his neck to look out the murky window.

The wind had subsided. It was snowing lightly now, and Charlie was outside, struggling with his crutches. On the snow and ice, he was trying to walk. He was trying to walk back to the cabin along the hard-packed path from the creek.

Time after time, Charlie fell down. Each time, he would pull himself up and try again. It hurt Jason to watch. But Charlie's eyes blazed with determination.

Then he took an especially hard fall. This time, he wasn't even trying to get up. Jason squinted for a better look, wondering what Charlie would do. Call for help, he hoped. Jason fought the impulse to run outside and help him to his feet.

Pressing his face against the makeshift window, Jason could see tears streaming down Charlie's face. Tears of utter frustration and rage.

Then Charlie struggled himself upright again, bracing with both crutches. He turned around and walked all the way to the creek and back.

"Where have you been?" Jason asked sleepily when Charlie finally came in the door.

Charlie flashed a huge smile. "Down to the Golden City. I met that Jamie you told me about. Prettier than the Gibson girl, if you ask me."

"Met Jamie, eh?"

"Said she was tired of waiting for you. Took a shine to me instead."

"I never said she was my girlfriend, Charlie."

"Didn't need to. Anyway, she prefers younger fellows."

"You rascal."

Charlie was giving King a good petting. The husky even rolled over to have his stomach scratched.

"Don't you steal my dog's affections away too."

As winter tightened its grip, Jason kept trying to locate the moose that would take them through till breakup. Dread was gnawing at him, but not so much that he didn't relish his return to the cabin every day. Charlie was there.

Charlie was a plucky customer, no doubt about that. His stump had fully healed, and it wasn't hurting him anymore. Getting around on the crutches had become second nature, and he'd even made good on his vow to split wood. It helped that it split so easily in the cold, almost of its own accord.

As the twilight failed with the dying afternoons and the interior of the cabin was plunged into gloom, Charlie would light a candle. They had plenty. They passed the hours talking, telling stories from Seattle and Chicago and all they'd known before.

Sometimes they played cards; other nights they took turns reading aloud to each other from the collection of *Scientific American* magazines on the shelf. The most recent issues were seven years old, but that didn't matter as long as they had something to read. Every one of them, they discovered, was inscribed in a fancy hand with the name of George Washington Carmack. This was the name, they both knew, of the American who was the world-famous discoverer of the Klondike gold. They concluded that they must be spending the winter in a cabin that used to belong to a man who was now fabulously wealthy and famous.

"Henderson was awful prickly on the subject of this cabin," Jason recalled. "Why would that have been?"

"His first name wouldn't have been Robert, would it? Robert Henderson?"

"It sure was."

"Well, he's sort of famous too."

"That prospector? You know something about him?"

"Robert Henderson's the Canadian who told Carmack to look where he did for the gold. I read all about it in the newspaper when I was in Dawson. But Henderson lost out."

"What do you mean, 'lost out'?"

"According to the story, Henderson met Carmack

and the Indians who were with him—two brothers named Skookum Jim and Tagish Charlie—at the mouth of the Klondike River. They were netting salmon there to sell to some miners at a camp downriver called Fortymile. Henderson told Carmack he was going back to work a creek that flowed into the Klondike—Gold Bottom Creek, he was calling it. Carmack asked him, 'Any prospects up there?'

"'For you, but not for them,' Henderson said, meaning the Indians. Carmack took offense, because he had been living with the Indians from Tagish Lake and Caribou Crossing for many years. In fact, these two men were the brothers of Carmack's wife."

"You're kidding. What a story. Go on!"

"Let's see. . . . After netting salmon for a couple more days, Carmack decided to go see what Henderson had found, and maybe stake a claim himself. He left the Klondike at Rabbit Creek, I think, and the three of them crossed over a ridge and down into Gold Bottom Creek, where they met up with Henderson and a couple others Henderson had told about his diggings. They were getting eight cents to the pan, which was supposed to be pretty good.

"While they were there, Skookum Jim and Tagish Charlie asked Henderson if they could buy some tobacco from him. He refused."

"Uh-oh. Carmack must've been boiling."

"Must have been, but he didn't say anything. Henderson asked if Carmack wanted to stake along Gold Bottom Creek, but Carmack said no. Then Henderson told Carmack he should try prospecting along Rabbit Creek on the way back. Carmack said he might, and, according to the story, he promised to send word back right away to Henderson if he found anything. Now, this is the good part—guess what Carmack found over there? He found the richest gold creek in the world! It got renamed Bonanza Creek, and one of its forks was named Eldorado Creek."

"Wait a minute. . . . You mean Carmack struck it rich and never sent word back to Henderson, like he said he would?"

"That's right. When he found the gold—or Skookum Jim did; nobody seems to know for sure—it was lying 'thick as cheese in a sandwich,' as everybody in the world has heard many times. Carmack filled a shotgun-shell casing with gold nuggets and flakes, the three staked their claims, and they headed down the Yukon to the camp at Fortymile. Carmack emptied his shotgun shell on the counter of a crowded bar and declared, 'Eight dollars to the pan!' Within hours, the camp emptied out. Everybody raced to stake close to where Carmack had made the discovery."

"And Henderson?"

"Three weeks later, he was working his claim when some men came over the ridge and started talking about the fabulous discovery at Bonanza Creek. Henderson was confused because he thought he knew the name of every creek within a hundred miles. They said, 'Right over the hill, here. Used to be called Rabbit Creek.'"

"Henderson must have been blistered. What'd he say? What'd he do?"

Charlie shrugged. "The way I heard it, Henderson said, 'That rabbit-eating malamute!' There was nothing he *could* do. The newspaper said there's been bad blood over it ever since."

"'Bad blood' must be putting it mildly. And to think, I met Henderson himself! No wonder he said he wouldn't have set foot in this cabin if I hadn't needed shelter. What about Henderson's own claim? It was so close, it must have been worth something. You said he was finding gold there."

"Henderson didn't even bother to keep working it, he was so disappointed over missing out on the big discovery. He signed it over to a doctor he owed money to for treating a leg injury. The newspaper said he was born the son of a lighthouse keeper on the Atlantic coast of Canada. He's been prospecting for twenty-seven years, starting when he shipped to Australia from Nova Scotia at the age of fifteen."

"No wonder he called himself a ghost. After all those years, he was so close. You know, you've got a memory for names, Charlie, and a way with a story. You should be a newspaper reporter."

"Maybe I could—back in Chicago."

"Why not?"

"You know, when this thing happened to me—my leg, I mean—I thought I wasn't good for anything anymore. I've been talking a lot to King about it when you've been off hunting."

"You have?"

"*He* never thought I was worthless. Never cared a hoot about how many feet I had. Then I realized *you* didn't either."

## TWENTY-ONE

Jason had been eating only enough to keep going. Without saying anything, Charlie also began to cut back. On the second day of December, as Jason returned from hunting, Charlie had a strange look on his face, worried and accusing at the same time. "I've been up in the cache," he said.

Jason was stung. "How'd you do that?"

"Like a monkey. The point is, Jason, we don't have the grub you told me we did. We can make it a couple months into the New Year, but how can we hold out until breakup? We're in a bad way, Jason, and you know what? I bet you never told my uncle George to leave me here. He just abandoned me. Isn't that the way it happened?"

"As he said, he didn't have any choice."

"Henderson didn't stay with you. Why should you be stuck with me?"

Jason's temper flared. "I'm not stuck with you, so don't say that I am. We're in this mess together, and we're going to make it through together."

Charlie looked relieved. "Don't be mad at me, Jason. Really, I'm not as worried as I sounded."

"Well, you should be. Now listen—I've been doing a lot of thinking, and I figured out what I need to do. Only twenty miles upstream, at the mouth of the Nordenskjold, there's an Indian village. I've made up my mind to go there and see if I can get some meat or fish from them."

"You couldn't get that far in a day—you'd have to camp out in the cold!"

"We don't have any choice. At the least, they'll tell me where the moose go. I'll have to take King along to pull the sled. You'll be all by yourself."

"Don't worry about me," Charlie insisted, his pride flashing.

"It might take me awhile to make this trip, Charlie."

"I'll be fine, if you'll just quit fussing over me. I'll keep the fire burning for you."

At first light, Jason packed the sled. As he produced King's harness, the husky bit some snow and leaped with excitement. When all was readied, Jason hooked King onto the sled's tug line, tightened the buckles on his snowshoes, and shouldered the packsack. Charlie handed him the rifle and they wished each other luck. Jason started out breaking trail, with King pulling the sled behind. At the edge of the clearing Jason stopped to wave, and Charlie waved one crutch high in the air and gave a cheer.

If I fail, Jason told himself, we're both dead.

As he passed the islands of Five Fingers rising from the frozen river, Jason looked back again. The landscape had swallowed the cabin up.

It was cold. Every time he breathed out, there came a crackling noise as the vapor hit the superchilled air. A cloud of ice crystals from his own breath enveloped him as he walked. It coated his eyelashes and clung to the earflaps on his fur hat, to the collar of his sweater and his mackinaw, as well as to the seams of his outer oilskin coat.

After several hours, he made himself stop. He had to make a fire, melt snow, make tea. It was so cold out that when he cleared his throat and spit, it froze before it hit the ground.

To arrange his birch bark and kindling and to strike a match, he needed the dexterity of bare fingers. He shucked his mitts and they fell to his side, attached by thongs he'd rigged for the purpose. A minute was the most he dared leave his hands exposed. Fortunately, his fire starter was full of oily resins. The birch bark flamed up with its usual aromatic black smoke.

The hot sugary tea felt good going down his throat. He could feel it warming him from the inside. King's pot of boiling water needed only half a minute to cool down enough for him to drink it.

Hastily Jason rewrapped his face with a wool scarf. Only his nostrils and eyes were showing, but still the hostile cold poured through. It poured through everything, including his wool-lined moose-hide mittens and his wool-lined sealskin mukluks. It was forty below and dropping, he guessed. When he tossed what was left of his boiling tea into the air, it made a great *whoosh*, turning into a cloud that drifted off barely above the ground.

Watching it go, the husky looked back at him quizzically.

"Oh, I'm full of tricks," Jason told him.

The sun appeared for an hour; then it was twilight again. Jason kept walking, but not fast. If he broke a sweat, he would freeze up.

When twilight was about to fail, he made his first camp. With a snowshoe, he shoveled away the snow where he would sleep, slashed spruce boughs for bedding, and made a pole-frame lean-to and roofed it with his tarp. He started his fire, dried out the linings of his mittens and mukluks, dried his socks—he planned on sleeping in all three pairs he had with him. A fine snow was falling as he set out with the ax to find dead wood. He'd need plenty to take his fire through the night.

There was no danger of freezing to death while sleeping. Every two hours he woke up shivering. Overhead, a brilliant aurora was writhing about like a curtain of magic rainbows. It was unspeakably cold. With a hooked stick, he would pull the unburned ends of logs onto the bed of glowing coals, then reach for his biggest logs to heap on top. In moments, his fire would be blazing again and he'd be warm enough, with the husky pulled close, to fall back asleep.

On the morning of the third day he crossed the Yukon to the site of the village at the mouth of the Nordenskjold, where he had stopped in the first half of October. Ominously, there was no smoke coming from the brush shelters.

"Hello!" he called as he snowshoed into the village. "Hello? Is anybody here? Anybody at all?"

Every structure, empty. Not a soul.

It took him a few minutes, standing dumbfounded, to formulate a theory. The Indians had been drying salmon when he was here. As soon as the last run was over, they must have left with their dogs and their sleds. That's why Henderson had been in a hurry to get here to do his trading. He knew they'd leave.

But where had they gone?

He had no idea, and they hadn't left a trace.

Had they left to follow the big animals, wherever they went?

Henderson, he remembered, was going to continue up the Yukon until he reached the Little Salmon, then follow it up into the mountains. Henderson wouldn't go where there wasn't plentiful game, not in winter.

The mouth of the Little Salmon, according to his map, was another twenty miles up the Yukon. He remembered a village there too. Perhaps that one was a year-round village. Maybe some Klondikers had made their winter camp there. What choice did he have?

Jason pressed on. The wind started to come up. Even a breeze seared like a hot iron. Soon it was howling. He wondered why his legs kept going, why he wouldn't let himself turn around. Late the next day he was still trudging forward, recalling a long walk he'd taken when he was no taller than Ethan's waist. He'd talked his brother into hiking to Mount Rainier. "I know I can do it," he'd pleaded. "Just let me try. You'll see." They'd walked for hours, eyes fixed on the peak, and the immense snow-clad mountain had never drawn closer.

He remembered the sudden realization that the mountain was much farther away than he had thought, and how he'd stopped to inform Ethan of his insight. "I think you're right," Ethan had agreed thoughtfully, and then they decided to turn back. It took years before he figured out that Ethan had known all along. After all, Mount Rainier was sixty miles away!

He looked up. Through the ice fog along the Yukon, he could make out the mouth of the Little Salmon and the shelters clustered there. Minutes later he found out that this village too was occupied only by profound silence. It seemed like he and the dog were alone in all the world.

Yet here was the track of a moose, a single moose, that had meandered among the shelters and up the white wastes of the Little Salmon.

He would follow that track. The moose pellets weren't steaming, but the track had been made since the last snow, only two days previous.

For two days he followed the moose track up the Little Salmon. Sometimes his attention lapsed and he would lose all connection to the dog behind him, the moose track, his churning legs. His mind would drift. It came to him what this endless moose chase was like. It was like the time he'd nearly killed himself at Duck Lake with his brothers watching.

He'd been trying to see how far he could swim underwater. Each time he'd broken his own record. On his last try he pushed himself farther and farther, simply refusing to come up for air. On the verge of finally bursting to the surface, he willed himself to keep going, and he blacked out.

By mule-headed stubbornness, he'd nearly killed himself that day. If his brothers hadn't been watching closely, hadn't hauled him out so quickly and thumped him sputtering back to life . . .

Jason stopped walking, heaved a sigh that turned into a puff of cloud. And you didn't learn a thing, he thought bitterly. Everything you've gone through, from stowing away on the *Yakima* to standing in this spot, has all been swimming underwater. *You did this to yourself.*

He should turn around and go back to Five Fingers, that's what he should do.

That's what he should do.

His eyes went back to the moose track, and he made himself concentrate. The track's significance came back. If he didn't get this moose, Charlie would never see his mother in Chicago and he would never see his brothers in Dawson City.

Or stake his claim.

The thought provoked a smile, which brought a sharp pain to his cracked lips. The gold rush! He'd forgotten all about it!

The gold rush, the Klondike gold rush. It had taken on the quality of a made-up story.

A gust of wind howling down the pearl-colored ice was about to reach him. He raised his mitted hands to block his face, and the gust passed by. The wind was replaced by a dead calm. The full moon was rising over the hoarfrosted cottonwoods along the river. From a great distance came the hooting of an owl.

The mountains were glittering with extreme precision in the cloudless, brittle-cold air. He was straining to believe in the gold rush. It didn't seem possible that a metropolis of sorts existed even farther north than this, several hundred miles farther north. That his brothers were there seemed even less plausible.

Nothing seemed real, especially the moose track he was following. It would only be real, he mused, if he could put a bullet through this moose and touch it as it lay dead.

He kept walking by the bright white light of the moon. His friend Jack could have read *The*

*Seven Seas* by the moonlight bouncing off the snow.

The next day, the moose track was joined by another, and now he was following two of the beasts up the frozen river.

He began to see mirages in the extreme cold: the sun squashed down and then fractured in two, a mountain range thrown up at an impossible angle. He saw Jamie's face suddenly painted across the sky. He'd forgotten she had those few freckles on her nose. He leaned forward trying to kiss the sky. Her image faded.

"You fool," he heard himself say.

Still, it was comforting to let his mind drift, to think of her. He recalled the wild look on her face as she was paddling that One Mile River.

It was a gray day, threatening snow. It had warmed up to twenty below or even ten, he guessed. He was in despair of ever overtaking the two moose. As he turned another in the endless bends along the frozen river, he stopped dead in his tracks. He realized he'd lost the will to continue.

Something up ahead, it seemed, didn't quite fit the landscape—a crude log cabin at the edge of a clearing and slightly above the river.

Another mirage.

But the mirage wasn't going away. Maybe there *was* a cabin there.

He trudged closer. Yes, it really was a cabin, an extremely small one. His heart leaped, but then he realized there was no smoke coming from it. Never mind, they could be away hunting.

Look inside this cabin, then turn back around.

Up close, he was stunned to see a beaten trail leading from the cabin to the river, and the unmistakable tracks of snowshoes. There really *was* someone here!

"Hello?" he cried. "Is anybody in there?"

There were no windows to peek through. A piece of heavy tarp served for the door.

As his mitten pushed the canvas to one side, light fell on two bearded men in fur coats and fur hats. Startled, Jason jumped back, lost his grip on the tarp. "Ho in there!" he cried out—no reply. Once again he pushed the tarp aside. The bearded men were sitting on rounds of wood, right there, right there in front of him.

A cooking pot was suspended over a fire, but the fire had gone out.

The men weren't moving, he realized, and in the next instant he saw why. They were frozen solid.

He cried out in terror, then clamped his mouth shut. If the moose were close by, he'd spooked them.

He dropped the canvas over the opening and retreated. He stood there frozen by fright, with the husky puzzling at him. All he could think about was that this was how *he* was going to end up, and Charlie too.

He had to get one of those moose.

Wait, there might be some way to identify these two. Their kin would want to know.

He crawled back inside with the two men sitting by the dead fire. There was a piece of shoe leather sticking out of the ice in the bottom of their cooking pot. This was what starvation looked like.

Here, on the log wall, was what he was looking for— a message scrawled in pencil and punched over a nail:

*Ours is the folly. Left Fort Simpson on the Mackenzie River. Seeking Dawson but lost. Too far, too late. Skin boat crushed by ice. Seen no game in weeks. Lack strength to continue.*

*God bless,*
*Samuel Whittaker and Villy Champlain*
*November 30, 1897*

They'd written this message less than two weeks before. They had died, maybe, only days ago. Where was Fort Simpson? Where was the Mackenzie River?

Jason folded the paper and put it in the pocket of his coat, then secured the tarp over the door to keep the scavengers out. He started upstream, more desperate than ever to catch up with those moose. But then it started snowing, and heavily. Before long, all trace of their tracks was obliterated.

"Let's go home," he told King.

He'd failed.

## TWENTY–TWO

It was New Year's Eve. All over the North, people found themselves in situations they could never have imagined when they set out for the Klondike.

A preacher from Farnellville, Ohio, and his daughter and a dying horse were stranded on the summit of Laurier Pass in the northern Rockies.

A circus with performing dogs and a tightrope walker were mired down on the Ashcroft Trail in the vast interior of British Columbia.

The wealthy stampeders who'd bought passage to Dawson City via the Bering Sea on the "all-water route" were seeing the year out only halfway up the Yukon, in the ramshackle shanties they dubbed Suckerville, where their two steamboats had been iced in for months. They'd left Seattle in the last days of July.

On New Year's Eve, twenty-one-year-old Jack

London was using a borrowed ax to chop the ice free from the spot where he and his partners drew water. Along with a number of other parties, theirs was wintering at the mouth of the Stewart River, sixty miles short of Dawson City. Suddenly the ax slipped in London's hands and struck a rock.

On seeing a chip in the blade of his ax, Merritt Sloper exploded. He was fed up with London's inviting every man he'd met over to the cabin to share the grub, which wasn't his alone, and to carry on his endless philosophizing. Jack London moved out to another cabin.

Six young Englishmen who'd celebrated the previous New Year's Eve at a resort in Switzerland saw 1897 out on the shores of Canada's Great Slave Lake, nine hundred miles north of the nearest town and still two thousand miles short of Dawson City. The newspaper and the merchants in Edmonton had trumpeted several "back door" routes to the Klondike that would take no longer than six weeks. For many traveling one of these all-Canadian routes, it would take two winters.

Few knew the geography of Canada's Northwest. It was terra incognita. On one of the supposed routes a man killed himself after pinning a note to a tree that said, "Hell can't be worse than this trail. I'll chance it."

Some used the mighty Mackenzie River, flowing out of the Great Slave Lake, as a highway to the north. Then they would trek west up its tributaries, the Liard at Fort Simpson, the Nahanni, the Gravel River, the Peel, or the Rat. The few who made it over the mountains that first fall were traveling so light, their survival depended on finding game. Some of them starved to death along the frozen tributaries of the Yukon before the year was out.

The stampeders were coming from every conceivable direction, but mostly they were still coming over

White Pass from Skagway and over the Chilkoot from Dyea. Even on New Year's Eve, some of them were in motion. No one knew that new strikes weren't being made every day in the Klondike, and so they kept pushing.

There'd been a land boom in Dyea, and it was already a town to rival Skagway. Piers from both towns extended a mile out to deep water. Plans were under way for a railroad over White Pass. By December, construction had begun on the first tramway over Chilkoot Pass.

On the Chilkoot it snowed seventy feet, and yet the stampeders kept climbing the Golden Stairs, each breath a rattling agony. They coughed until their ribs cracked, and still they kept climbing. During a single night two men hacked one hundred and fifty stairs in the ice up the final pitch, and collected eighty dollars a day in tolls.

The tent restaurants and tent hotels at Canyon City and Sheep Camp and the Scales did a big business, as did Soapy Smith's confidence men, who hiked the trail with bogus packsacks filled with straw, preying on the stampeders.

Frame buildings had risen at Lake Lindeman and Lake Bennett, housing hotels and restaurants, but tents far outnumbered them. There were tents for hot baths, cafés, hotels, barbershops, chapels, saloons, casinos, real-estate offices, and bakeries, as well as the sleeping tents of thousands upon thousands of Klondikers.

At least a thousand more Klondikers were building their boats downstream along Tagish Lake, Marsh Lake, even as far as Lake Laberge. No matter the hardship— the closer they could get to the head of the pack, the better.

All celebrating the New Year in the cold, confident of riches and anxious as racehorses for breakup.

In Carmack's old cabin near Five Fingers, Jason and Charlie were in desperate straits but celebrating the last day of the year nonetheless. Charlie had baked a peach bannock for breakfast in honor of the occasion. As they were savoring it bite by bite, Charlie suddenly blurted out, "Knock, knock, who's there?"

Jason jerked his head around toward the door. "Is someone here?"

With a grin, Charlie said, "It's a game."

"Oh . . . okay . . . who's there?"

"Gretta."

"Gretta who?"

"Gretta long, little doggie, gretta long."

Jason laughed. "Ethan and I played this when I was two feet tall."

"Knock, knock," Charlie began again.

Jason had to smile at how much his friend was enjoying this diversion from the grim reality of their predicament. "Who's there?"

"Thistle," Charlie said.

"Thistle who?"

"Thistle be a lesson to us."

"I've got one for you," Jason announced. "Here goes. Knock, knock."

"Who's there?"

"Ima."

"Ima who?"

"I'm a-goin' hunting. See you before 1898 gets here."

Jason was about to add what he was going hunting for, but the idea would sound crazy. Besides, he felt superstitious about saying the name of the animal aloud.

It was an animal he hadn't even thought of hunting until the day before, when a remembered piece of conversation had suddenly given him hope.

The joking mood was broken. Deadly serious now, Jason fed King one of the small tins of fish, then stuffed his pack with everything he might need. He dressed in every layer he had and went out into the cold with the rifle and the husky, snatching up the long, thin pole he had fashioned the previous afternoon. He was going to try to find Henderson's bear.

It was crazy, but he had to try it. As he snowshoed upriver, he kept going over and over in his mind what Henderson had said about the bear. The bear had eaten from the moose, then had gone into hibernation. "The den is probably close by," Henderson had said. Henderson had said something else too, about the Indians watching where the bears den so they could come back and hunt them when they were asleep.

If he could only find the den.

The bear would be asleep. Killing it couldn't be that hard.

Spiraling away from the place where he'd earlier found the moose carcass eaten by wolves, Jason began probing with the pole. He stared at every irregularity in the snow, scratched under every log, under every overhanging rock. Nothing looked like a den. Did he even know what a den would look like? How would he know one?

"King," he whispered. "Sniff him out for me. It's a bear I'm looking for, a bear to feed the three of us."

New Year's Eve and here he was, starved from six weeks of half rations and staring at every little hillock, trying to imagine an opening that wasn't there. Finding the proverbial needle in the haystack would be easier.

He'd been away from the cabin about two hours. The sun was finally making its appearance in the south, about to make its brief run along the hilltops.

He stopped in his tracks. You're getting too cold, he told himself. You need to make a fire.

King took a few steps in the direction of the cabin, looked back.

"You're probably right, boy. We should go back. What do I know about hunting a bear, especially one I can't see?"

Then it hit him.

You've only looked on the east side of the river! Bears can swim, can't they? Of course they can. That bear could have crossed the river and denned on the other side. Get warmed up, make some tea, cross the river, and look over there.

You have to keep trying.

## TWENTY-THREE

Jason started across the frozen river. Where to look?

He snowshoed up the far riverbank and scanned the low, rolling hills. A den could be anywhere or nowhere. Despite what Henderson had said, the closest den could be miles away.

It was just after midday when King came upon widely spaced gashes in the soft snow and began to sniff the track of the small, leaping animal that had passed this way. A fox? Jason wondered.

Why had the animal been leaping?

Now King was investigating the leaping tracks in the direction the animal had come from. The husky seemed so intent, Jason followed. Within twenty yards, the leaping tracks led back to an overturned spruce. When the big spruce had toppled over, it had raised a mound with its roots.

By the time Jason got there, King was sniffing at a tiny hole in the mound of snow. It was apparent from the tracks leading to the hole that the fox had come here at an unhurried pace, then gone leaping away. Had something spooked the fox?

The hole was knee-high, only two or three inches across. There was a bit of old moss showing, coated thick with frost.

Suddenly the husky's ears went down flat. King sniffed a few times more, then backed away, tucking his tail between his legs. His ears alternately stood straight up, and flattened back down. King approached the hole again, wagging his tail cautiously.

"Let me try," Jason whispered, and knelt by the hole. He put his nose to it, smelled nothing. He put his ear to it, listened hard. He detected the muffled yet unmistakable sound of breathing.

Heart thundering, he backed away.

It's not necessarily a bear, he told himself.

But it could be. What else could it be?

He took off the packsack and pulled out the ax. He'd better have the ax ready in case the rifle jammed or misfired. Here was the box of extra ammunition. Yes, there's a shell in the chamber, and it will take only half a second to lever the next one into place.

Now what?

Henderson had made light of the way the Indians hunted a bear in its den. If only he'd said how it was done.

Maybe he didn't know.

Henderson seemed to think it was a black bear, from a print he'd seen. The thought of a grizzly scared Jason to death. Even a black bear, he guessed, could weigh four hundred, six hundred, even eight hundred pounds.

The bigger the bear, the more meat.

Poke it with the long pole and make it come out? Be ready to shoot it as it came out—that's all he could figure.

Jason took off his snowshoes, and he used one of them to clear the snow away within ten feet of the little hole. He needed room; he didn't want to be thrashing around in the snow.

With the snow cleared away, he put his packsack on the bare ground and laid the ax, the rifle, and the ammunition on the pack, where it would be close at hand if need be. With the sharp back end of a snowshoe, he began to enlarge the tiny opening in the snow.

The husky sat close by and watched intently as he worked more quickly now with the blunt front end of the snowshoe. He exposed an opening in the earth, two feet in width and three high. King whined and his ears lay down flat.

Barely able to breathe, Jason leaped back for the rifle and stood ready, but there was no sound from within, at least none that he could hear. King began to whine once more and Jason whispered, "It's okay, boy. If there is a bear in there, it's what we came for. He'll be so sleepy, we don't have anything to worry about."

Cautiously, he crept back to the entrance, knelt, and peered inside with the rifle ready. An arm's length away, the tunnel was plugged with vegetation—chunks of moss and grass and twigs from blueberry bushes.

With his heart in his throat, Jason reached for his long pole and began to feed it through the plug of vegetation. The plug gave, but the pole was stopped only six feet away. He stood and angled it slowly down. If he touched the bear with it, he wanted it to be very gently, at least at first.

But the pole was stopped again, and he realized that the den must angle away from the entrance tunnel—to the right rather than the left, but at an angle he couldn't negotiate with the straight pole.

Even if he wanted to, he couldn't jab the bear with this pole.

What now?

Jason stood ten feet back from the entrance, on bare, firm ground, and began to shout for the bear to come out. He got the husky barking too, but as much as they carried on, nothing came out.

No bear.

Had he really heard something breathing in there?

With the rifle propped up and ready, the ax too, he cleared the plug in the tunnel, pulling the vegetation out with the blunt end of the snowshoe. Then he knelt and put his ear to the entrance once more.

He heard nothing.

Maybe he'd only imagined breathing. Or else the bear was awake now, and staying quiet as could be.

If so, how was he going to get the bear to come out?

Fire? Smoke the bear out?

He'd used up the birch bark he had with him and there was no tinder in sight. The clumps of moss he'd pulled out of the den were frozen solid.

Even if he could make smoke, it wouldn't pass down into the den.

His eye fell on a runt of a spruce close by, dead and limbless, bent in a curve. With that pole he might be able to determine where the bear was, exactly—if there *was* a bear.

With the rifle ready and his eyes remaining on the entrance, he backed away, leaned his body against the dead spruce, and broke it off at ground level. Once again he probed the tunnel, this time with the curved pole.

It came to rest against something soft, something that gave. He jabbed at it while keeping his eye on the rifle.

As if a fish had struck, the pole jumped in his hands, and there came a growl.

The husky whined, backed away. Jason retreated, grabbed up the rifle, and stood ready, finger on the trigger.

The bear didn't come out.

He hollered again, at the top of his lungs, and got the husky barking again, but still the bear wouldn't come out.

"I'm not going in after you," Jason hollered.

Was there another way to dislodge the bear?

Maybe there was. From the length of the pole he had fed into the tunnel, he knew how far away the bear was. From the curvature, he knew where. He didn't think the top of the den was that far underground. Maybe two feet.

He had an idea, and he might as well try it. It had to be today. Overnight, the bear might move, now that it had been disturbed.

Where he determined the roof of the den to be, Jason cleared the snow away, then began to chop at the frozen ground cover with the ax, one eye always at the entrance, and the rifle ready. Surely the sound and the vibration would scare the bear out its tunnel. If it didn't, he'd expose the bear from above and shoot it.

An hour later he finally broke through. Twilight was deepening. He was running out of time.

It was too dark to see down into the den. He enlarged the hole with a heavy swing of the ax, then several more, until the hole was eight inches across, but still he couldn't see and he couldn't detect motion. He kept looking to King, on his haunches ten feet back from the tunnel entrance, for a sign that the bear was finally going to come out.

The opening he'd made was big enough to shoot through. It was only a matter of determining direction. Laying the ax aside, he shucked his mitts and took up the rifle, kneeling and probing with the tip of the barrel, a foot, two feet inside. As soon as he felt something, he'd fire.

With a sudden, powerful jolt, the rifle was knocked from his freezing hands, and it fell inside the den. In the next moment the bear erupted, head and shoulders, through the roof of the den, growling and snarling and clawing at his leg with an outstretched paw.

In a blur, as Jason lunged for the ax, the bear roared and pulled itself up and free onto the snow. Jason raised the ax, held tight, and dealt the big bear a slicing, punishing blow to the head. The husky was barking wildly. With a glance sideways, Jason saw a second black bear, not full grown like the first but nearly, come charging out of the tunnel, directly at King. The bear went up on its hind legs, claws high, as the husky darted toward it, then away.

Just then a *third* bear, a twin of the second, came snarling out of the den.

It was all happening so fast, like a nightmare.

The bear in torment from the ax wound was almost on him before Jason realized it. He whirled and came down with the butt end of the ax head hard on the bear's back, at the midpoint of its spine. The big bear folded, paralyzed.

When Jason looked again he saw, only for an instant, the husky and the second bear in a snarling embrace.

Suddenly the third bear was charging, not at the husky, but at him.

The charge was nearly instantaneous. All but on him, the bear pulled up short as Jason raised the ax handle to shield himself. The bear stood high on two legs and slashed at him with daggerlike claws.

Jason saw his chance and swung the blade of the ax across the bear's belly. Its bowels came pouring out onto the snow. But the bear wasn't down, and it kept slashing, reaching his skin through two coats and everything underneath. Jason swung again, this time at the bear's chest, and had to leap away as the bear crashed to the ground.

The second bear was giving King a ferocious mauling. Jason ran as fast as he could to get there. He raised the ax, but the bear spun and slapped the ax end over end into the deep snow.

The ax was lost and he was weaponless, and now the bear turned its full roaring attention on him.

In desperation Jason leaped for the den, where his only other weapon lay inside. But as he dived and clawed his way inside the tunnel, the bear was tearing at his boots.

As fast as he could, Jason bellied and elbowed his way downward into the widening den. It was dim, but he could make out the rifle by the light from the hole he had chopped in the roof. He lunged for the rifle, with the enraged snarling of the bear coming right behind. He whirled around with the rifle and fired point-blank into the oncoming bear. In the confines of the den, the explosion was deafening. A second shot, and the bear lay still at last.

Jason pulled himself out through the roof of the den. The snow was bloody all around, bright red and horrible. The bear he had maimed was moaning, but there was no sound from the husky.

He went to King's side and found him still breathing, but he was a sight Jason would never afterward be able to put very far from his mind. The husky had been disemboweled, just like the bear Jason had cut with the ax, and he'd lost a frightening amount of blood.

This was mortal, Jason knew. King had only moments to live.

Jason lay down in the snow next to him, and their eyes met. The dog lifted his paw and placed it on Jason's hand. "King!" Jason whispered as his chest heaved with a sob that came from the deepest part of him, where he mourned his father and his mother and couldn't call them back either.

The dog knew how to die, pouring love through his eyes into Jason's. The great husky's amber eyes glazed over, and then he was gone.

PART THREE

# The Golden City

## TWENTY-FOUR

All around the cabin the snow was gone, and the early flowers were blooming. But the Yukon River was still in the grip of the ice, even though the sun was high in the sky and streaming sunshine nearly around the clock.

When the last week of May arrived, Jason and Charlie knew the ice would have to yield soon, and within a few days it did. It began to groan, and to crack, and to move, but just as quickly it seized up again and there was no sound or movement at all.

A few days later, when it moved again, blocks of ice weighing countless tons ground against one another and jostled for position—and went nowhere. They locked together downstream from the cabin and formed an immense dam. A temporary lake was forming in front of their eyes as the river level rose and floated the field of shards higher and higher up the banks.

187

They shook their heads and looked at each other. "Are we safe where we stand?" Charlie asked.

"You'd think so," Jason answered. "This cabin has been here for years."

A few minutes later, the ice was rising above the Yukon's bank.

"I'm not so sure," Jason said. "We better move our things, and fast."

They dragged the canoe to higher ground first, then rushed into the cabin and packed their gear into pack-sacks and flour sacks, and hustled it up the low ridge above the cabin. All the while the ice was rising higher and higher, beginning to crush the bushy alders along the bank. They barely had time to save the last of the bear meat.

Then came a sound like a thunderclap and, moments later, the entire river of ice was on the move again. "The dam broke!" Charlie yelled.

From the knoll above the cabin, they saw the chaos of ice resume its inexorable march downriver, shearing and grinding and making a thunder. Berglike pieces larger than the cabin went tumbling by. Along both banks of the river, tall cottonwood trees were snapping off like matchsticks.

The dam must have solidified again, because the ice once more came to a standstill, and the temporary lake began to rise again. The ice floated higher and higher, until the river was lapping at the door of the cabin and they thought it surely couldn't rise any more.

It rose, relentlessly, until only the roof of the cabin was showing amid a surging sea of ice. The cache appeared to have no legs under it.

When the dam broke the second time, it sounded like the end of the world. They watched the ice go out finally in a catastrophic surge, taking the cabin and the cache and hundreds of trees with it.

Jason had his eye on a five-foot piece of log, neatly sawed at both ends, that had lain behind the cabin since the first week of January. The log was bobbing down the Yukon now, holding its own with the ice on the beginning of a long journey. Jason pointed to it, remaining silent. Seeing where he pointed, Charlie nodded, recognizing the log. "There he goes," Charlie said solemnly.

Both were streaming tears. Jason was remembering how they'd tried to dig a grave in the frozen earth and failed. Yet they couldn't bear to burn King's body or to leave him out in the open where he'd be exposed to scavengers. They'd sawed a five-foot length from a downed cottonwood and split it down the middle. With the hatchet and the ax, each of them had chipped a hollow in his half of the log, as if they were making two miniature dugout canoes. When they were done, they pieced the halves back together with the husky's body inside, then bound King's coffin securely with rope, around and around.

They were about to lose sight of the log downstream. "The King of the North," Jason whispered, "that's what you were. Good-bye, King—I'll never forget you. I hope you make it all the way to the Pacific Ocean."

The next day, the last day of May, they decided it was safe to load the canoe and start downriver. Charlie boarded, nimble as a cat, and stowed his crutches. With a glance back at where the cabin had stood, Jason got in the stern and pushed off. He couldn't help shouting, "Klondike or bust!"

If his brothers were down at Dawson, it couldn't possibly turn out a bust. It had taken him nearly a year and over five thousand miles to understand the relative value of gold. He wouldn't trade his brothers—Charlie either—for the wealth of George Washington Carmack.

Still, he couldn't help wondering if there had been fabulous new discoveries made since last fall. If so, he'd be among the first to stake.

"Let's paddle," he said. "Who knows how many are on our heels."

Their canoe shot downstream like an arrow.

Upriver, thirty thousand stampeders were expecting breakup at any moment. They'd been champing at the bit all May.

Time was of the essence, and they were primed for a five-hundred-mile race.

On May 29, the ice began to go out on the lower lakes, Laberge, Marsh, and Tagish. Eight hundred boats hoisted crude canvas sails and men pulled on the oars until they thought their backs would break.

On May 31, the ice went out from Lake Bennett and the One Mile River and Lake Lindeman, and now the entire armada—7,124 boats of every description—was on the move at last. The Mounties estimated that the cargo included thirty million pounds of solid food.

Down the lakes came the most bizarre flotilla ever assembled, from dugout canoes to Huck Finn rafts, catamarans, innumerable skiffs of twenty to twenty-five feet, scows as heavy as twenty tons floating horses and oxen, even a small steamboat that a man and his wife had packed piece by piece over the Chilkoot and reassembled.

When the winds died out, sometimes everyone stopped rowing, and the race was suspended without a word spoken. Someone with a deep, booming voice would begin to sing a song of home, Virginia or Scotland or even Australia. As the song carried across the lake, all eyes lifted from the mirror-calm surface spangled with sails to the snow-clad peaks and the azure skies above. Men and women wept at the beauty, at the thought of the hardships they had endured and the loved ones they had left back home.

They knew they were a part of something grand. Mad, but grand.

As the flotilla approached Miles Canyon, a bottle-neck of Olympian proportions developed. Word came back that one hundred and fifty boats had wrecked in the preceding forty-eight hours, and five men had drowned. Some had attempted the canyon and rapids below without even scouting them from the shore, they were in such a hurry.

At the foot of the White Horse Rapids, some were in despair, while others scurried to salvage what they could of their boats and belongings. Jacob Jackson of Des Moines, Iowa, who'd toted hundreds of pounds of seed over the Chilkoot, saw his dream die when his boat swamped in the White Horse. He had come north not to find gold but to grow hardy vegetables and sell them to the stampeders.

Some of the boats waiting above Miles Canyon contained commodities, luxuries, even perishables freshly packed over the passes to be sold at the highest possible prices in Dawson City. Thirty or more boats were carrying eggs by the crate; one had a crate of live chickens. One was loaded with tinned milk, one had a milk cow, one was carrying dozens of cats and kittens, and one had newspapers only a month old that told of war with Spain. An Italian fruit merchant was transporting sixteen thousand pounds of cucumbers, bananas, oranges, lemons, and candy.

Colonel Sam Steele of the Mounted Police, who'd rushed down from Tagish Lake after envisioning the bottleneck, learned of the drownings and immediately stopped all traffic at the entrance of the canyon. Unless order could be quickly established here, the river could take a far greater toll than the seventy lives the Palm Sunday avalanche had exacted on the Alaska side of the Chilkoot.

A giant of a man in scarlet jacket and yellow-striped trousers, the superintendent spoke to the throng huddled at the entrance of the canyon: "There are many of you who have said that the Mounted Police make the laws as they go along, and I am going to do so now, for your own good. Therefore, the directions that I give shall be carried out strictly. No boat will be permitted to go through the canyon until the corporal is satisfied that it has sufficient freeboard to enable it to ride the waves in safety. No boat will be allowed to pass with human beings in it unless it is steered by competent men, and of that the corporal will be the judge."

As everyone knew, Steele's fine of a hundred dollars for anyone breaking the rules would be enforced.

Steele's regulations worked. Many decided to portage their outfits, but many others ran the canyon and the rapids, almost always successfully.

In the first half of June it was nearly impossible, from Bennett to Dawson City, to be out of sight of other boats. Suddenly it was hot, as hot as ninety degrees, and mosquitoes hatched in the moss of the forest floor by the untold billions. Frank Cushing of Buffalo, New York, tried some of the mosquito repellent he'd packed over the pass—ten thousand bottles, which he planned to sell for ten dollars apiece. The lotion raised such horrible blisters on his skin that he threw the entire shipment into the Yukon.

The mosquitoes descended on the stampeders with a vengeance. For some Klondikers, this was the last straw. Tensions that had simmered through the endless winter suddenly erupted as the men were on the verge of reaching their destination. At the mouth of the Big Salmon River, ten partners divided everything they had onto ten blankets, sawed their scow into ten pieces, and reconstructed ten individual boats.

Of the thirty thousand floating toward Dawson, only several hundred arrived before Jason Hawthorn and Charlie Maguire. Most of these had spent the winter sixty miles upstream of Dawson City, at the mouth of the Stewart, which had become known as Split-Up City for all the partnerships that had come to grief there.

As Jason and Charlie paddled those last miles above Dawson, there wasn't a boat in sight, upriver or down-river. They had passed the mouth of the White River the day before, and they knew they were close. At last the canoe rounded a rocky bluff and there it was, under-neath a dome-shaped mountain with a landslide scar: a gleaming miniature metropolis in the wilderness, a city of white tents and frame houses, hotels and warehouses, just beyond a fast-running clear stream entering from the right—the Klondike.

"Great day in the morning," Jason declared. "It's the Golden City! We made it! Now, where are my brothers?"

Charlie was pointing to the lettering across the back of one of the warehouses. It read HAWTHORN BROTHERS SAWMILL.

## TWENTY-FIVE

Jason cleared his throat and spoke up. "I'm looking for a job."

The baldheaded clerk in the tent office at the sawmill's entrance peered over the rims of his eyeglasses. "We need men, but the owners expect me to hire experienced hands sixteen years and older."

"I turned sixteen this spring."

"All right, I'll grant you that, but have you ever worked in a sawmill before?"

"No, but I always wanted to. Back in Seattle it was the same thing—you had to be sixteen, and I wasn't old enough yet. I heard the owners are from Seattle. Are their names Abe and Ethan?"

"Abraham and Ethan, yes."

Jason's heart leapt. It wasn't a mistake. The sawmill

194

didn't belong to some other Hawthorn brothers.

Trying not to spoil his own fun, Jason didn't allow himself the merest grin. "I knew them in Seattle. I'd be much obliged if you'd ask them if they'd give me a job—they won't regret it. You could tell them that my father worked in a sawmill, and my brothers too. It runs in my family. Tell them I also have a lot of cannery experience. I'm a good worker."

"You seem pretty determined."

"Oh, I am. Would you mind telling them all those things, and tell them I'm waiting out here, hoping to hear about the job?"

The clerk seemed slightly amused. "I will," he said. "I'll find one or the other, and tell him everything you said."

The minutes dragged like hours as they waited.

"Tink-eye," Charlie said when he couldn't stand the tension any longer.

"Tink-eye who?"

"Tink I gonna pop."

Just then, around the side of a mountain of logs, here they came—Ethan with his full beard and burly logger's physique, and straight-as-a-pine Abe, trailing with his slight limp.

"Jason!" they cried, eyes enormous with astonishment. They slapped him on the back as Charlie hopped to the side on his crutches.

"We sent your passage in a letter, only a few days ago!" Ethan exclaimed. "On the first boat out, care of Mrs. Beal. How in the world did you get here?"

With a grin, Jason replied, "Very gradually. I left Seattle only three days after you did."

For a moment neither of his brothers could speak.

He was sure Ethan would make some joking remark, but both were dumbfounded. They stared at him, then at Charlie.

"What happened?" Abraham asked finally. "Tell us everything."

"My friend Charlie and I . . . we both ran into a few difficulties. . . ."

Their eyes went to Charlie's leg, then back to Jason's weather-beaten face.

"We're sourdoughs," Charlie put in proudly. "We wintered at Five Fingers. Your brother saved my life."

They kept nodding all the while, Abe worrying his mustache, Ethan beaming. They were still looking Jason up and down, still shaking their heads. "You've grown like a kelp weed," Ethan marveled.

Abe said in measured tones, "It's been a long time since you left home, Jason. You're practically a grown man, and you favor Father."

"Am I ever glad to see you two," Jason said softly, giving way to tears he could no longer hold back.

Now his brothers were surprised all over again. They'd never seen him cry.

At midnight, in the log cabin his brothers had built on a high back street, the June sunset was still blazing and his brothers were still asking about the Chilkoot and the winter. At last Jason was able to steer them back to the present. He said, "I still can't believe I'm part owner in the Hawthorn Brothers Sawmill."

"And rightly so," Abe replied in his sober manner. "You helped stake us. We three Hawthorn brothers own a fifty-one percent interest in this sawmill."

With his tongue in his cheek, Jason looked from one to the other and asked, "How did *we* accomplish that?"

"The two of us who got here first," Ethan began in the same vein, "thought we were going to strike it rich within a matter of days. We hotfooted it out of town and found some ground to stake, but, as you can see, you aren't looking at two of the kings of Eldorado."

"We starved out fast," Abe continued. "Several thousand men had had a year to prospect the entire country before we got here. The worthwhile ground had already been staked."

"So we found jobs at a sawmill," Ethan said. "It was what we knew how to do."

Abe leaned forward in his chair. "The owner of the mill was a man named Joseph Ladue. He owned all the ground under Dawson City. He'd filed on it within days of Carmack's discovery and has been selling off parcels of land for houses and businesses all this time. He wanted to start more sawmills, and he liked our work, so he staked us on this one."

"Ladue didn't want the trouble of managing it," Ethan put in excitedly, "so he made us the majority owners. That way he could be sure we'd make a go of it."

"Is the gold still coming in from the creeks?" Jason asked. "Will all this building keep going?"

Ethan burst into a hearty laugh, his impish green eyes shining. "There's no end in sight! Fabulous amounts of gold are coming out of the creeks every day. Just Wednesday, a man shoveled twenty thousand dollars out of his claim in twelve hours."

"Can we go see the diggings? Charlie and I want to see Bonanza Creek and Eldorado Creek."

"Sure—let's all take a wagon ride out there in the morning."

"What about the sawmill?" Jason objected. "Don't shut down work for my sake."

Abe raised a wry eyebrow. "The lately arrived part-ner doesn't want to see a production slowdown. . . ."

Ethan laughed, then explained, "Tomorrow's Sunday. The mill is inside the city limits, and Dawson has blue laws—everything closes up." Ethan pulled out his watch from his vest pocket, opened it up. "I should have said, *Today* is Sunday—it's six minutes past mid-night. Six minutes ago, the opera house and the saloons, every business in town closed its doors. The Mounties are strict. Last week a man was fined for mending his fishing net on the Lord's day."

As the lumber wagon clattered across the bridge over the Klondike, Abe let the horses crop at the grass. Then he started the team up the Bonanza Creek Road. Jason was expecting a landscape to match his glorious image of the fabled gold creeks, but what came into view was a scene of utter devastation. A battlefield that had under-gone a year's shelling couldn't have looked bleaker.

As far as the eye could see, the hills had been stripped to the ground, looking all the more naked for the occasional tree sticking up along the ridges. Cabins and tents and lean-tos, privies and caches were scat-tered randomly among immense mounds of dirt and gravel, as if they'd been dropped by a cyclone.

Along the valley floor, not a vestige of greenery remained. A creek splashed its way through ditches and diversions, among heaps and heaps of bare gravel and much more machinery than seemed likely here at the ends of the earth: rockers and boilers, steam engines, winches, pumps, and hoses.

Here was the greatest human anthill in the North. On all sides men were toiling with insectlike industri-ousness. Some were winching buckets of ore from vertical shafts that riddled the area, while others shoveled dirt and gravel into the sluice boxes—rickety knee-high wooden chutes running with diverted streamlets.

"Here it is," his brother Ethan announced grandly. "The richest placer in the world. What do you think, now that you're here?"

Jason grinned, shook his head. "I'm remembering a newspaper article I read during the first week of the rush. It was about a new company called the Trans Alaskan Gopher Company. They were offering stock at a dollar a share and said they were projecting to make ten dollars a minute. The idea was that the gophers were going to dig up the gold."

His brothers burst out laughing; Charlie too.

Jason said, "I guess most of these men aren't the claim owners. Are most working for wages?"

"You bet they are," Abe agreed.

Jason grinned. "I'm thinking how much I love the smell of sawdust."

All the while, his eyes were scanning the ranks of the miners close and far. He was looking for a girl among them, a girl with hair dark as a raven's wing, alongside a man with a beard that was gray and big enough for birds to nest in. Would he run across them in Dawson? Had Jamie and Homer already gone home? They no longer had their farm to go home to.

Within a few days the Yukon rose with the spring runoff, spilled over its banks, and flooded Dawson to the tops of the door frames. It was a close call, saving the machinery and the logs at the sawmill, and Jason was in the thick of the fight. The cabin on the hillside stayed high and dry.

As the waters ebbed, another sort of flood arrived—

that of the world's adventurers, twenty thousand almost at once and more to come. They found Dawson City knee-deep in muck.

Not that the muck slowed anyone or anything down. The boats kept coming, new buildings kept rising, and the sawmill kept working around the clock. It was light all night—no reason to shut down, except for Sundays. Jason threw himself into every job at the mill, worked ten hours a day, gave it every ounce of his determination.

It was the greatest feeling in the world being back with his brothers, working alongside them as an equal. He was so proud about the mill. If only their father could see them now!

It was different for Charlie. He'd become a valuable assistant to the bookkeeper, but his mother and Chicago remained at the forefront of his mind. Charlie decided he wanted to head back. The Hawthorn brothers told him that by August they could afford the tickets to get him all the way home.

Evenings and Sundays, Jason and Charlie walked up and down the streets of the city. Dawson was spilling in all directions; the tents of the stampeders checkered the hills with white even on the opposite shores of the river. The two of them stood on the riverbank along Front Street and watched the boats pour into town until they were three thick all the way up and down the Yukon, with barely room for the stern-wheelers from downstream.

Two of those steamboats, *Seattle No. 1* and *May West*, had been stuck in the ice all winter at a place eight hundred miles downriver that the passengers called Suckerville. They'd been 314 days on the "all-water route" from Seattle, and they were angry as hornets.

"Serves 'em right," Charlie said, "for trying to do it the easy way."

Of the Klondikers arriving from upstream, thousands rushed out of town to stake claims and try their luck with pick and shovel and gold pan, even though prospects were said to be poor. Many went to work for wages to earn their passage home. A few pushed off almost immediately for the fourteen-hundred-mile float down the Yukon to St. Michael, where they hoped to catch a ship.

Thousands simply milled around Dawson, gawking at the sights. It was a marvel simply to be here; they knew they'd never see the like of this again. Even though it was summer, they wore their fur hats like a badge. They were too worn-out by what they'd gone through to do much of anything but stroll. Every half hour they'd bump into someone they'd met during fall, winter, or spring along the trail, and they'd stop to swap stories.

It was a golden summer, though few found gold. There was a sense of pride that helped to alleviate the disappointment, a sense of satisfaction in having made it, which would be impossible to explain to folks back home.

Dawson was a carnival, a perpetual carnival. Jason and Charlie laughed their way through the auction of the first "cackleberry" laid in Dawson City—the egg sold for five dollars. They saw a miner from the creeks pay fifteen dollars for an eight-month-old newspaper that was soaked with bacon grease.

They came across a milk cow—a man had actually floated a milk cow into Dawson, and he was selling the milk at thirty dollars a gallon. Thirty dollars a gallon! They met another man who'd floated a slew of cats and kittens down the Yukon and was selling them for an ounce of gold apiece.

You could buy anything from clothes to fresh grapes to ice cream. Charlie was especially keen on ice cream. Strangely, perfectly good rifles were selling for a dollar each, and they were available by the hundreds. No one had any use for them anymore, not here. Pistols were strictly forbidden. Possession of one would have resulted in a quick "blue ticket" out of town. Nobody seemed to mind that there wasn't a shooting a day, like in Skagway. There weren't any shootings at all. Robberies were unheard of. The Mounties had succeeded in keeping the rush peaceful on the Canadian side of the border.

Jason and Charlie ran into the wizened old man Jason had met hauling the grindstone over the Chilkoot on his back. He was set up in a tent, sharpening miners' picks or shovels for an ounce of gold apiece. An ounce of gold was worth sixteen dollars!

One day they had their photograph taken in a tent studio by Eric Hegg, the photographer Jason had met on the Chilkoot. Fastened to the canvas walls were photographs Hegg had taken along the way—of the endless chain of Klondikers going over the Chilkoot, of boats in the White Horse Rapids. There was even a picture of Hegg's own sled drawn by his five longhaired goats.

Along Front Street one day, Jason came across the old-timer he'd met in the boxcar rolling across the prairies of North Dakota. The grizzled veteran of the '49 rush and many others was starting up the gangplank of a departing stern-wheeler.

"Old-timer," Jason called. "Remember me?"

The old man squinted at him, then broke into a smile. "Sure do."

"Did you strike it rich this time?"

"Sure didn't," the old man replied with a grin.

"Me neither, but I don't give a hang."

"Oh?"

"Doesn't matter, because . . . I have seen the elephant!"

The old-timer waved his hat, laughing, and clambered onto the boat.

Always, Jason kept his eye out for Jamie, but after a few weeks had gone by, he'd pretty well given up. The Dunavants would have been broke, he realized. They'd probably left a few days before he got to town, on the first steamboat downriver.

On the last Saturday in June, Abe and Ethan took him and Charlie to see a variety show at the Palace Grand Theater. His brothers told them it had been running all winter and was the most popular show in Dawson. The show was enjoyable enough, mostly singing and dancing, but the last act—"The one you've all been waiting for"—shook him like a leaf. When the curtain was drawn, there stood Jamie at the front of the stage in a splendid white dress, black hair shining, with her father, Homer, in the background, scribbling on a notepad in front of a mock log cabin!

"That girl's been performing all winter," Ethan whispered. "She's the Princess of Dawson."

As Jamie struck a pose and began to speak, a profound hush came over the audience:

> "When you can't climb a step more, my friend,
> Don't look at the ground, don't ever give in.
> Lift your eyes to the peaks, you'll shed your cares,
> There's glory there, at the top of the Stairs.
> Lift up your eyes, don't ever despair,
> There's glory there, at the top of the Stairs.

*To give in, my friend, would be such a pity,*
*For it's not the gold that counts—*
*It's reaching the Golden City.*
*LIFT UP YOUR EYES!"*

When Jamie shouted the last line and raised her hands dramatically above her head, the entire theater responded with a roar and with deafening cheers. Jason looked around, dumbfounded by the power of the chord Jamie had struck. It was reverberating in every heart. He'd seen her father writing this very poem that day, on the way over to Dyea, as Homer had looked from his notepad to those snow-clad peaks!

Jamie went on to perform a dozen more of her father's poems. They were tales of the rush, rhyming narratives of the trials and tribulations and the longings that everyone in the house had experienced. Often they spoke of home and hearth and loved ones far away.

At the mere mention of home, coming from the lips of this lovely young girl, hundreds of grown men, hardened-looking men, would burst into tears, some of them weeping shamelessly. As Jason scanned the crowd, his eyes suddenly locked on a familiar face. To his astonishment, it was his friend Jack London.

## TWENTY-SIX

Jack was staring beyond the girl to the poet, whose only role in the performance was, alternately, to reflect and scribble a few words on his notepad. Jack's eyes were blazing with an intense fire, and there was a quiet sort of joy lighting his face.

With the last standing ovation of the evening, Jamie and her father disappeared backstage. Jason was still stunned. Jamie was here! He could see her after all.

First, he'd run for his old friend Jack before he disappeared in the crowd.

London beamed with sudden recognition. "You made it!" he exclaimed, pumping Jason's hand. Jack had lost several more teeth, and his cheeks were puffy, but those blue-gray eyes still radiated his infectious good nature. "I've been wondering when I'd come across you, Jason. Did you find your brothers?"

205

Jason pointed. "They're right over there."

"Good, good. . . . Do you see that big fellow standing next to your brothers, the one talking to the boy with the crutch? Know who that is?"

When Jason shook his head, Jack said, "That's Big Alex McDonald, one of the kings of the Klondike! Owns shares in fifty claims, they say, and many of the buildings in town. You mustn't have wintered in Dawson, I take it."

"I wintered at Five Fingers, with that boy you pointed out. That's my friend Charlie."

"What held you up?"

Jason smiled at the way Jack had put it. "A moose did."

"I'd love to hear *that* story. . . ."

"What about you? Where'd you winter?"

"At the mouth of the Stewart. I staked a claim on a creek nearby, then floated on down to Dawson right before freeze-up. I spent about six weeks just taking in the stories here, then tromped back on foot to the Stewart in early December. Was it ever cold! Fifty degrees below zero."

"What about your claim? Strike it rich, did you?"

London pulled a small vial out of his shirt pocket. "Got it right here."

Jason scrutinized the bottom of the vial. There was gold dust there, all right, a few flakes—not much.

"Four dollars and fifty cents," Jack said with a laugh. "Won't exactly see me home."

"You're leaving?"

"Tomorrow. I'll be floating out with a couple other fellows on a scow. In three weeks or so we ought to make it to St. Michael. From there I hope to find work on a ship back to California."

Jack had been sitting all this while, and now

he attempted to stand up. "Whoa," he groaned.

"What's the matter?"

"It's this accursed scurvy; I've been in a pitiful way all winter. But I need to go home anyway. . . . My father was bad sick when I left."

They arranged to meet the next day, and then Jason bolted onto the stage. At the dressing room door he was stopped in his tracks by a man in a tailcoat who sported a waxy handlebar mustache. "I'd like to see Jamie Dunavant," Jason said, all out of breath.

The man's thin eyebrows rose haughtily. "Wouldn't everybody?"

"You don't understand—I'm an old friend."

"I'm sure you are."

"All you'll need to do is tell her my name. . . . Wait a minute—I'll write it down for you." Jason pulled the stub of a thick lumber-marking pencil out of his shirt pocket and wrote his name on the back of the evening's program, along with "Hawthorn Brothers Sawmill."

"Just show her this, and tell her I'm out here," he said. Then he added, "I'd be much obliged. I met her back in Skagway. . . ."

The man shrugged, nodded curtly, and disappeared inside. A minute later he was back, without Jamie. "Well?" Jason asked.

"You have to understand," the doorman said. "A lot of people would like to see Miss Dunavant. She's a very famous person."

"You mean . . . she won't see me?"

"She simply can't take the time. I'm sorry, but you'll have to run along, before I—"

Jason left without another word. He was burning with embarrassment.

In a daze, he found himself back with his brothers

and Charlie. They asked where he'd been; he mumbled something about a friend named Jack.

Still reeling, he followed his brothers and Charlie to the rooms of Big Alex McDonald. McDonald was a simple, slow-talking bear of a man with hands the size of hams. His lavish accommodations, all decorated with art and gilded mirrors and ostrich feathers, polished brass and cut-glass chandeliers, seemed so unlike the man who inhabited them. Big Alex, upon seeing Charlie at the theater with his crutch, had sought him out after the show and asked what had happened to him. "I want you to see my fishbowl," Big Alex had said after hearing Charlie's story.

Now that everyone was in his rooms, it was apparent that the fishbowl Big Alex had been talking about was a huge bowl of etched glass displayed on a fancy marble stand. It was filled to the brim with gold nuggets.

"Now, how soon are you going to be able to get back to Chicago to meet up with your mother?" Big Alex asked Charlie.

"The Hawthorns here are going to help me, soon as they can afford it. I'm hoping by August I'll be leaving."

"But you'd rather go sooner, I take it."

"Yes, sir, I'm pretty ready to go home."

"Well then, son, you just reach into that fishbowl there and help yourself."

Charlie looked at him uncertainly.

"Help yourself!"

Charlie reached in and took a few nuggets in his palm. One was big as an acorn.

"No, no!" Big Alex said, waving his hand. "I mean fill both trouser pockets full as you can get 'em, then your shirt pockets too. Gold means nothing to me, lad. Nothing!"

• • •

Still numb from the way Jamie had treated him, Jason went to the docks the next day to see off his friend Jack. He spotted London aboard a crude scow that was little more than a planked-over raft of logs. Jack was busy mending the attachment of the big sweep oar at the stern, but he waved Jason aboard.

Unlike the Princess of Dawson, Jason thought bitterly.

Jack showed him around the scow. "That's a sleeping shed in the middle here, and look—our yacht's even got a mud hearth for cooking. Yessir, I'm on to the next chapter of my life."

"I'm sorry you're not staying, I really am."

"It's a grand country, Jason, and it'll stay in my blood. But I'm determined as ever to find a way to live on my own hook. I keep telling myself that it must be possible to make my living with my mind instead of my muscle. I never told you this, but what I'd really like to be is a writer."

"Like Rudyard Kipling or Mark Twain?"

Jack tossed back the shock of hair that was always falling in his eye, and he laughed. "Exactly. Why not? Why not Jack London? Maybe I can mine some other kind of gold out of this whole experience."

Here came Jack's boat mates, two fellows who looked like scarecrows. "Let's shove off," one of them grunted.

It was time to say good-bye, shake hands, and disembark. Jason untied the heavy rope holding the scow and tossed it aboard. The ungainly craft began to drift. "Good luck with the mill," Jack called. "In the years to come, I'll be picturing you up here."

"I'll be here. And I'll be looking for your books!"

Jason watched his friend disappear around the bend, working that big sweep oar.

The good-byes were coming too fast. Three days later he saw Charlie off on a steamboat fixed up fancy as a wedding cake. At the last, Charlie vowed he'd come back once he'd seen his mother, and that he'd live the rest of his life in the North with the Hawthorn brothers. Whether he really would see Charlie again, Jason wasn't so sure.

Jason threw himself into the work at the mill. Business was booming, and his brothers said he was doing the work of three men. He never told them that it was helping him keep his mind off a girl named Jamie.

He didn't go back to the Palace Grand Theater to see her perform; he even avoided the streets of Dawson on Sundays, when the mill was closed. He didn't want to turn a corner and suddenly run into her.

In the fourth week of July, Dawson was electrified by the news that Soapy Smith had been shot dead in Skagway. A throng assembled in front of the theater to hear the particulars read. The man who'd killed him, in a one-on-one gun battle on July 8, was a surveyor named Frank Reid. In the exchange, Reid was hit; he underwent an operation but died from his wounds. Eleven of Smith's gang, including Slim Jim Foster, Charles Bowers, Old Man Tripp, and Kid Barker, were being shipped to Sitka for trial.

Cheers went up, including Jason's. Many around him, he guessed, had also been victims of the gang. He remembered how they had swindled Jamie's father.

He wondered if she was here, at this moment. He found himself scanning the crowds for her, not knowing how he'd feel if he saw her face. But he didn't see her.

Finally it happened. Two weeks later he was stacking lumber at the mill when he saw the flash of a billowy white dress from the corner of his eye. He straightened his aching back and turned, to see her right there in front of him in the lumberyard.

"Jason!" she cried. "It's so good to see you!"

He didn't know what to say. What was she doing here?

"Hello," he said awkwardly.

Her face wilted. "What's the matter?" she said, looking all around, as if she'd find an explanation in the lumberyard.

A dozen men, including his brothers, were standing still as statues, looking at them. Not only was it a girl; they all knew who it was. "Let's go where we can talk," Jason said, and he led her around a mountain of logs and down to the riverbank.

All the confusion had his heart going like thunder. "I don't know if you ought to sit down," he said without looking at her. "You'll get your dress dirty."

"Oh, that doesn't matter," she said. And then, as if to prove the point, she plopped down on dirt rather than rock.

Now he felt even more confused, struck by lightning and dumb as wood. He glanced at her hazel eyes, the few freckles on the bridge of her nose. She was prettier than ever. He didn't know what to say. He didn't want to tell her how bad she'd made him feel.

"So how long have you been here, Jason?"

"Since practically the first of June."

"And you never came to see me?"

"Oh, but I did," he said quickly. "I saw your show, and it's fantastic. I thought I was going to die, you were so good."

"It's all Father's words," she said, blushing. "But I

don't understand—why didn't you come talk to me after the show?"

"I did," Jason said, "but they told me you didn't want to see me."

"That's crazy! Who told you that?"

"A man standing outside your door. I gave him my name, even wrote it down for him."

"Oh my gosh! No wonder you're acting so strange." Her face lit up. "Well, that explains everything. Nobody ever told me you came to see me. Jason, I didn't even know you were here in Dawson until just a few hours ago. I found your name written on the back of an old program, on the floor behind some props backstage. Why, just imagine if I hadn't found it. I might never have known you were here!"

A crushing weight had been lifted from his heart. He threw his arm around her shoulder and gave her a squeeze. He just couldn't help himself. "Nothing's like I thought it was," he said, beaming. "You really *are* the same—only your hair's longer now."

"So is yours! What did you mean about not getting here until June? When we left you off at Dyea, you started out ahead of us. I thought all you had to do was get over to the other side, to catch your brothers where they were building a boat."

"It's a long story. . . ."

"And I want to hear every word of it."

With a grin, he said, "I saw you and your father run the One Mile River in your canoe."

"Really, you did?"

He gestured as if he were stroking with a canoe paddle. "You were phenomenal—the girl from Swift Water! Did you paddle straight to Dawson, like you planned, and beat freeze-up? What about Miles Canyon and the

White Horse Rapids? Did you portage at Five Fingers?"

She laughed. "We beat freeze-up, but we took our time along the way gathering berries and rose hips, and Father got a moose, which we dried in strips just like the Indians do. We made a smokehouse to dry all the salmon we'd caught. We portaged Miles Canyon, but we ran Squaw Rapids and the White Horse. What a ride! And when we got to Five Fingers, we ran it, down the channel closest to the right shore."

"Five Fingers . . . I know that area well."

She reached out and took his hand. "It's so wonderful to see you, Jason. It's been a rare day I haven't wondered how you were doing. And then to find out you and your brothers own one of the new sawmills!"

"Dawson has a future, Jamie. . . . We're going to stick. I've got a new home in the North. I didn't even know what I was looking for until I found it."

A bittersweet smile crossed her face. "I love it every bit as much as you do, Jason. But we're leaving."

"Leaving—but why? Your show is so successful. I don't understand."

"That's just it. The show is so successful, we're going to do a North American tour: Seattle, Portland, San Francisco, then all across the continent, ending in New York City."

"That's wonderful," he said blankly.

She'd heard his disappointment. "I'm so proud of my father, Jason. To see the effect that his words have on these audiences . . ."

"How soon are you going?"

"The next steamboat. It should be here within a week."

## TWENTY–SEVEN

These few days were the happiest in his life, but more fleeting than a northern wildflower. Word came all too soon that *The Pride of the Yukon* had reached Fortymile and was expected in Dawson City within twenty-four hours.

There was time for one last triumphant show at the Palace Grand Theater. The line for tickets stretched three blocks long and around a corner, but Jason and his brothers didn't need tickets. They were seated in a special box with Big Alex McDonald, Joseph Ladue, and Edith Van Buren, the niece of the former President of the United States, who'd come upriver as a tourist and erected a lavish pavilion across the river from Dawson.

For the occasion, Homer had written a new poem, entitled "My Heart Remains in the Northland," which

Jamie recited as their finale. Though Jamie's eyes
seemed to encompass every Klondiker in the house,
they came to rest on Jason for the last stanza:

> *"For though I roam in far-off climes,*
> *In my heart, dear friend, I'll be counting the time*
> *Till winter fades and breakup nears.*
> *So look for me when first flowers appear,*
> *I'll be on the first boat, and it will feel so grand,*
> *Because, don't you know—*
> MY HEART REMAINS IN THE NORTHLAND!"

With her last line of the season, Jamie threw up her
hands in her inimitable fashion, and the audience rose,
shouting "Bravo! Bravo!" and tossing bouquets of wildflowers onto the stage.

As *The Pride of the Yukon*'s whistle blew the following morning and Jamie was about to board, she confided
that she'd written that last stanza herself. "We'll be back
for the summer season as surely as the swans and the
geese," she promised.

"And I'll be standing right here on the dock," Jason
told her.

"Who knows, maybe then we'll stay. . . ."

"Who knows," he repeated bravely. It seemed such a
long, long time.

A few minutes later he watched *The Pride of the
Yukon* disappear around the bend. So much was
slipping away—Jamie and Charlie, Jack London, the
trusting amber eyes of King, the chain of Klondikers
ascending the Chilkoot. . . .

Jason lifted his eyes to the mountains towering

above the Golden City. He'd come so far, and he'd made it.

He turned back to the sawmill and broke into a run. Everyone at the mill was racing to make the lumber for a new hotel. He was needed there.

## AUTHOR'S NOTE

*Jason's Gold* goes back to my childhood in Alaska in the 1950s—my memories of the winter darkness and the northern lights and rusting gold dredges. In the three decades since, I've recited "The Cremation of Sam McGee" countless times around wilderness campfires and have felt the powerful pull of what its author, Robert W. Service, called "the Spell of the Yukon."

In the midnineties I finally saw the settings of the fabled Klondike gold rush for myself, from Skagway, Alaska, to Dawson City, in Canada's Yukon Territory. I didn't know then that I would write a Klondike story, but as my wife, Jean, and I were hiking, rafting, and visiting museums, the jade green waters of the upper Yukon River were seeping into my subconscious, as were the personal histories of those who took part in what Canadian historian Pierre Berton calls "one of the strangest mass movements in human history." In 1997, stirred by the centennial celebrations taking place in the North, I was taken with the idea of going on the rush imaginatively, one hundred years later, while dramatizing it for my readers.

I am particularly indebted to Pierre Berton's extraordinary history, *Klondike—The Last Great Gold Rush,* first published in Canada by McClelland and Stewart in 1958. Another "gold mine" was *Chilkoot Trail,* by David Neufeld and Frank Norris (Lost Moose Publishers, 1996). It has a fine text, accompanied by numerous Eric Hegg photos of the rush. I would also point interested readers to *Women of the Klondike,* by Frances Backhouse (Whitecap Books, 1995); to *The Miners,* by Robert Wallace (Time/Life Books, 1976); and to *The Book of Jack London,* by Charmian London (Mills & Boon, 1921).

Many of the characters in *Jason's Gold* are actual historical figures. They include Soapy Smith, "Old Man" Tripp, "Reverend" Charles Bowers, "Slim Jim" Foster, Captain William Moore, Eric Hegg, Robert Henderson, George Washington Carmack, Skookum Jim, Tagish Charlie, Col. Sam Steele, Jacob Jackson, Joseph Ladue, Big Alex McDonald, Edith Van Buren—and, of course, Jack London, as well as his partners, Captain Shepard, Merritt Sloper, Fred Thompson, Jim Goodman, and the latecomer, Tarwater.

Twenty-one-year-old Jack London sailed from San Francisco on the *Umatilla* on July 25, 1897. He was grubstaked by his sister, Eliza, and her husband, sixty-year-old Captain Shepard, who was accompanying London. At Port Townsend, Washington, London and Shepard transferred to the *City of Topeka,* bound for Juneau. For the last leg they hired Indian canoes to take them to Dyea, as reported by Fred Thompson, who kept a diary.

London himself did not keep a journal of any kind, it seems, until he was floating out on a scow from Dawson City to the Pacific in June 1898. From his own accounts, it was only as he was leaving that he thought of turning his failed attempt to strike it rich into grist for his literary ambition. I have endeavored to portray Jack London's history as accurately as possible, down to the scarlet long underwear he wore while toting his one hundred and fifty–pound loads up the Chilkoot Pass on a sweltering day in late August. Jack disposed of Captain Shepard's outfit after the older man turned back, for health reasons, before ascending the pass. It occurred to me that in my novel, Jack London could convey his brother-in-law's outfit to my protagonist, who would be in need of one.

London and his partners launched their *Yukon Belle* onto Lake Lindeman on September 16, as in my story, and barely escaped ice-up on Lake Laberge. He was the steersman when his party ran Miles Canyon and the White Horse Rapids. That Jack London lingered to earn money by taking dozens of other boats through, as reported in some of the histories, is probably a myth. His wife and biographer, Charmian London, reports that he took one other boat through the rapids, and not for profit. London and his partners were in a deadly race to cover the next several hundred miles before ice-up and find winter quarters. A voracious reader, Jack London packed along books by the authors I mentioned. One of the volumes was *Das Kapital*—in addition to being an individualist, London was a passionate socialist. During the winter he borrowed Rudyard Kipling's *The Seven Seas* from someone; the record doesn't say who that was. Clear as day, I pictured my protagonist giving it to him.

Fictional characters in *Jason's Gold* include Jason

Hawthorn and his brothers, Abraham and Ethan; Mrs. Beal; Kid Barker; Charlie Maguire; and Jamie and Homer Dunavant. As the reader might guess, Homer Dunavant was inspired by Robert W. Service, though at the outbreak of the gold rush, Service was headed for Mexico, and wouldn't arrive in the Yukon until the next decade. Charlie Maguire is based on William Byrne, a teenager who froze his feet, had both legs amputated at the knees, and was abandoned by his uncle and others as they made a desperate upriver retreat from Dawson City in October 1897. Byrne survived the winter, alone, in a shack near Five Fingers.

The cabin where Jason and Charlie wintered in this story—also near Five Fingers—was a real cabin that had been occupied years before the rush by George Washington Carmack. His library there included issues of *Scientific American.*

Several of the elements of my story that might seem pure fiction are based closely on research. The two frozen men Jason encountered on the Little Salmon are based on an account of two corpses discovered on the upper Porcupine River, a far northern tributary of the Yukon. These men and many others died attempting one of the "back door" routes to the Klondike.

Jason's desperate struggle with the wounded moose, as well as the specifics of his den-hunting experience, are based on actual incidents. To this day, Athabaskan natives in Canada and Alaska still continue their ancient practice of hunting black bears in their dens. I learned that the depth of a bear's sleep, as well as its willingness to leave the den when roused, varies a great deal. I would recommend *Hunters of the Northern Forest* and *Make Prayers to the Raven*, by Richard Nelson (University of Chicago Press, 1973 and 1983, respectively).

I hope that some of my readers will want to discover the upper Yukon country for themselves. Dawson City today is a thriving year-round town of two thousand. Though a mother lode of gold was never found, small placer mining operations continue. Visitors might buy a nugget, but they come to marvel at the compelling and epic human drama that was played out there.

The Klondike gold rush, which began with Henderson's and Carmack's discoveries in late summer of 1896, continued through the summer of 1899. Of the approximately one hundred thousand people who set out for the Klondike, around forty thousand made it to Dawson City. Of those, only half are thought to have even looked for gold. Of those, only four thousand are thought to have found gold. Of the four thousand, only several hundred struck it rich.

Durango, Colorado
July 1998